ADAM JORDAN

No Man's World

Book II - Rupture

First edition

Editing by Courtney Andersson
Cover art by Jeff Brown Graphics

This book was professionally typeset on Reedsy.
Find out more at reedsy.com

Contents

Chapter 00-Prologue

A scarlet sunset warmed the world and even its people, no matter how cold-blooded. A woman pulled a grey scarf over her head as the wind poured in through the open windows of her sports car and filled the fabric with air. The flapping cloth did not bother her, but the slowing of the traffic did. The freeway began to descend down into the mouth of a man-made cave, an entry point to the interlocking underground networks that mostly relieved traffic in the dense modern age. Several levels allowed vehicles to pass through more efficiently than in the days before the mass overhaul. As she descended deeper, artificial light replaced the dimming natural source. The honking of horns and echoing of expletives grew tiresome, so she switched on the radio and found one of her favorite songs halfway through its run. She tapped her fingers with the beat and nodded her head, clearing her mind and seizing the day. A smile graced her lips as the music rekindled the spirit of her youth. She was a single woman now; her fiancée nowhere to be found for the latter part of a month. For weeks she had sulked and questioned herself, but today was different. As of today, she would live a life without stress or worry—one dedicated to herself.

As she contemplated the near future, she found the further

slowing and buildup of cars unusual. Suddenly, the earth cracked and roared, and the artificial lights flickered, then died altogether. In the pitch-black, she heard nothing until a fury of dust burst through the tunnel, mighty and sharp. The emergency lights of the tunnels belatedly turned on and struggled to illuminate the dark through the clouds of dirt and sand. It was then that she realized she was bleeding from her forehead, and that her car was partially crushed by others both in the front and back. The old lady ahead did not look responsive, and the car behind was abandoned.

Her hearing returned to her. Car alarms, kids, women screaming, and men crying and shouting echoed in the tunnel. Fights and scuffles surrounded her, while the smarter ones stayed in their cars, petrified and likely coming up with all manners of theories as to the cause of the quake. Times were unstable. They were at war.

The woman, squished in her car, was relatively unhurt. She couldn't feel pain at that moment, but knew she was not wholly alright. She remained frozen as fainter bombs shook the world above. She tried to switch the radio over to the news, but it was dead. The tunnel's security system alerted, "Emergency Lockdown Mode," repeatedly with its feminized computer voice.

Unbeknownst to the woman, outside the tunnels an array of white-blue lights had made sure that the bombs stopped: advanced technology hushing primitive warfare.

Months later, or maybe years, the woman stalked the putrid tunnels like a panther with a blackened steel pike. She was on the lookout for another convenient pop-shop at a waystation intersection. She had survived off of bags of chips, candy, and granola bars, but with what little she did find, the substance was usually a net loss when compared to the effort of the hunt.

The earth trembled from above. She'd grown used to the tremors, though they grew louder and more consistent each time, and they were always accompanied by a zapping static now. Maybe it was the time that had passed, or how on guard she'd had to be against rapists and rats, but the outside hum felt almost . . . rejuvenating.

More time passed, and the dark twisted and tormented her mind further. She forgot what the sun or moon looked like, and she spoke to herself in resentful, belittling words. One day, she awoke to find that the zapping tremors were gone. Even if she wanted to check, she did not know how to escape the labyrinth of tunnels. She was tired, hungry, thirsty, and blind.

At some point, she stumbled upon a rickety ladder, covered in dust and soot and spiderwebs. What else to do but to climb? She climbed and climbed until her head hit a rusty roof. Reaching up, she felt a metal wheel. She turned the wheel with all her strength, limited as it was, and managed to push open the hatch. As she climbed through, the black remained unlit, but she felt another ladder continuing up.

She climbed through several more layers of dark tunnel and road, opening latch after latch until the final one blinded her with its release and a breeze embraced her. The light was so hot and white, she almost lost hold of the iron grips. She blinked painfully, and her sight eventually returned, though fuzzily at first. As she crawled outside, shaking and broken, she thought she had climbed to a different planet. The world around her was unlike anything she had ever seen before. High up in the heavens, she saw a burning sun and a violet moon paired against the azure sky.

Chapter I- Scorched Earth

An alien forest collapsed and burned, dying in the midst of morning. A dragon of smoke ascended to block the sun. Half a mile north of the blaze, a group of six watched the flames of their arson. The group consisted of a pale young man, a capable elderly woman without teeth, a twitching fellow with tired bags under his eyes, a man with a sack over his head that had two eye holes cut out of it, a short and stout bearded man who wielded a heavy flamethrower with a shark's face painted on it, and the slim and tall leader with greasy black hair and a shabby jacket. The leader's eyes were shut, and he was reiterating rhetoric to his flock.

"This world is a vile attempt at the end of humanity. It is not our world, but a reminder of what we have lost; an infestation, a disease. In order for humanity to rise again, we must purge this planet of its foreign filth . . . scorch the landscape and be reborn amongst the ashes." He ended with his eyes still shut. Suddenly, a twig snapped in the surrounding wilderness, and shadows began encroaching from behind tree and bush, branch and thicket, and vine and slope. The arsonists looked around in a panic while the leader remained still with his eyes sealed shut.

The great fire patiently crept closer in the background,

enjoying the consumption of forest.

"Come on out, friends. Share with us the delights of liberation," the leader announced aloud. Not a moment later, a platoon of heavily armed survivors emerged from the surrounding veil, snickering and bloodthirsty. "Hello brothers, have we staggered into your territory?" the cult leader acknowledged politely.

"You sure have . . . and you set our backyard ablaze. Why would you do something like that?" a young warlord asked as he approached through his company with a leash in hand, dragging the slack through the dirt. Attached and following without any resistance was a chained reptilian monster topped with a spiked shell. The creature's tail was coiled up and weighed down by chains behind it. The warlord's face was dirty, and his attire was hardened by dried blood. A pair of gruesome blades that looked like the fangs of some primordial cat hung off his belt, and a black Beretta M9 rested in his shoulder holster. The scars scrawled onto his exposed skin told stories of his sanguinary past.

It was Slugger, leader of the Last Men, and his beloved pet Marge. The arsonists and their leader directed their attention toward him.

"You think you can just—" Slugger stopped abruptly as he glanced into the leader's wide-open eyes. "What the fuck? Who are you looking at? Can you even fuckin' see?" Slugger barked. The leader remained silent; his eyes were black and permanently directed inward, stuck in place. "Seriously . . . I completely forgot what the fuck I was gonna say. So, your eyes are just, stuck like that?" Slugger continued.

"I have strabismus, but I can still see . . . and what I see is a sham," the leader replied calmly.

"Hey now, you're talking about our home," Slugger snapped with the ends of his mouth curling up.

"Your home is gone; buried under this altered landscape, this . . . abomination of science. Don't you see? We wash it away with fire and dig our old world out from below, so civilization can rise from the ashes like a phoenix," the cross-eyed leader implored.

"Honestly, you're probably saying some crazy ass shit, but I can't even pay attention with your eyes like that. Are you looking at me right now?" Slugger antagonized. The arsonist leader regarded him quietly. Slugger eventually lifted his gaze from the man and scanned the rest of the group. When his gaze fell on the pale adolescent, he smiled. "This one. You've crossed into our lands before. I seem to remember giving you the utmost hospitality, and this is how you repay me? 'Course, we sent dogs after you to find out where the rest of you were hiding, but you got away, and that was gonna be that. But not anymore. You messed up. This is our world . . . and now none of you get to be a part of it."

"Heretics! Come to test our fire?" the bearded man bellowed and aimed his flamethrower at Slugger, who simply let go of Marge's leash. The chains dropped with a weak chime, muffled by the dusty impact. He then clicked his tongue twice, and his beast charged at the threatening target.

The stout man torched the dragon, but it leaped through the flames, unscathed, and pounced on him. Marge then began to eat the man's face while he screamed; part of his beard caught fire and smoked and smoldered like a nest. The twitchy arsonist with bags under his eyes attempted to run away during the commotion, but a hidden sniper took him down. The rest of the small group cowered—with the exception of their eccentric leader.

"No one's leaving!" the deranged warlord exclaimed with delight.

"Brother. Why do you slay your own kind?" the cross-eyed leader asked.

"Because your own kind can be your worst enemy," Slugger answered, darting his gaze toward the leader.

"But we are not your enemies. We are your friends," the leader responded politely.

"These are my friends." Slugger opened his arms wide, referencing his vast gang behind him. "He came into our land." Slugger pointed to the terrified adolescent. "Then he went crawling back to you after I gave him a sack of food and tells you to come here and burn it down to the ground? What kind of friend is that?" Slugger asked, playing along.

"Why do you fight so hard for a world that isn't ours anymore? We are here to liberate you, all of you. Our world will return when this rot is cleansed," the cross-eyed leader implored with true conviction and a touch of desperation.

"Our world will return once civilization returns you fuckin' moron. We are building toward the future here. You guys could have been a part of something bigger, but instead you wanna whine and bitch about what you lost," Slugger retorted. "You make me sick . . . and I still don't even know if you're even fuckin' looking at me!" he yelled, then drew his hand cannon and shot the elderly woman in the head. He then proceeded to shoot the arsonist with the sack mask through the brain as well, leaving the leader and the youth as the only remaining two of their group. Marge stopped feasting and looked toward her master.

The young man, barely in his twenties, collapsed to the

ground and began to whimper and cry. His leader remained still, his blank face lacking emotion as he contemplated the unknown. "Tie 'em up; we're gonna roast 'em alive," Slugger commanded as he walked over to secure Marge's leash. The creature nuzzled him lovingly, smearing fresh blood on his shirt.

Over the course of thirty minutes, the gang constructed a pyre and tied their captives together in the center. "Please, no! I'm sorry! Let me help you guys!" the young man pleaded, paler than before.

"Shut the fuck up you pussy and die like a goddamn man," one of Slugger's men hissed in his ear. The youth, sentenced to die, whimpered and further dampened his piss-soaked pants. His leader remained silent with his crossed gaze straight, focused on nothing in particular.

Slugger's men poured the last of the gasoline while others laughed and anticipated the execution. "Burn slowly, you pieces of shit," Slugger muttered before tossing a lit match onto the epicenter of the pyre. The flames erupted immediately and began to eat at the pair's flesh when the wood wouldn't satisfy their endless appetite.

The young man screamed as his skin melted off of him, but the leader welcomed his fate, and with all his strength announced his final thoughts, "All of you will suffer worse than us, and you will forever be empty and dead, lost without a home."

Slugger threw an empty canister of gas that struck the man in the head, silencing him; the audience erupted into laughter at the scene, while a few remained hushed in discomfort. Afterward, a brief moment of silence was interrupted as the two bodies began to crackle and pop as the fire overwhelmed their carcasses. Slugger sniffed the air of his victory and smiled, holding his hard crotch gently.

"Hey Boss, what do we do about that?" asked one of his loyal henchmen, a man with thick black dreads and a large scar over one eye. He was pointing to the forest fire heading their way.

"Goddamn it, Willie. Sometimes you just gotta give me a moment," Slugger complained. Willie remained quiet, awaiting orders. "Fuck it, it's not gonna reach us back home. Let's roll out."

Willie hesitated, then objected, "It's gonna hit my home." Slugger raised an eyebrow as the man continued, "All the outposts out here are gone if we don't do something."

"What do you suggest, we spend the next few weeks battling this thing? Digging fire breaks that might not even work? The whole goddamn forest is gone. No, fuck this, we're going home. Take your crew if you want to salvage whatever you can but I don't know what the fuck you expect me to do," Slugger stated. His henchman scowled and turned to gather his crew. Slugger's eyebrows grew heavy and he scoffed.

Suddenly, he was reminded of six faces; young faces whom he deemed his responsibility. One stuck out in particular: a pair of brown eyes rippling like wavelets in a murky pool peeking out from an overdressed guise. He froze and contemplated his options, but finally decided that it was up to them. No more would he run to their rescue. They must be strong; they must be tested.

In slight turmoil, the leader tugged at his war beast and led his gang through the woods back toward the road. The sun dropped, but they continued to tread through the moonless dark to outrun the glowing blaze and the grasp of the smoke. They eventually found the decrepit road along with their vehicles, guarded by a smaller party, and mustered the caravan to full speed.

Chapter II- The Crack

The party stormed through the land until the breach of dawn. Eventually, they came upon an abandoned campsite that they frequently used. It had a fire pit ready to be refueled and lit. The caravan pulled over, and the tired men poured out to get to work starting a fire and preparing food.

Marge was panting and dripping dehydrated drool, a pinkish green froth. Slugger unhooked her from her reins and patted her on the head. He wandered back to his convertible-made-sleigh and popped open the trunk, took out a human arm—presumably belonging to one of the arsonists—and tossed it to his pet. Slugger then filled a large bowl with some musty water and placed it on the ground beside her meal. Lastly, he uncoiled her tail. It was longer than her body and writhed and thrashed around once he loosed it, but everyone knew to stay away; they all knew that one lash was enough to take skin from bone or a head from shoulders, even with the resistance of the loosened chains.

Afterward, he joined his men in the heavy labor. When everything was in place, the tyrant and his troop began to cook raccoons, rats, and an assortment of alien critters on sticks. Breakfast was spent mostly in silence, as was the remaining time spent recuperating for the upcoming home stretch of their journey. The men rotated taking naps while the vast column of smoke from the distant fire crept closer.

Marge breached their rare moment of relaxation when, with no provocation, she wailed and moaned and slapped her immense tail against the ground repeatedly. The chains clanked like a terrible tambourine player. "Oh, goddamn it, not again!" Someone complained from amongst the crew.

"Hey, fuck you!" Slugger barked and stood up while the creature continued to cry and smack her tail. "You guys know how she gets without her Homer, and we're almost back, so I don't want to hear another fucking word about it," he finished while Marge's howl shrieked through their deranged and starved minds.

Slugger was able to soothe her and attach her back up to the car with care and patience. She then let him wind her tail back into a tight coil—after he massaged it—with the same black steel and leather that comprised the reins. "Let's roll!" Slugger shouted, and the disgruntled men resentfully mobilized.

The caravan barreled down the road with Slugger at the helm. His 1970 Stingray convertible wore a dingy orange-red paint, like the glare of a late sun. The engine had been removed and the frame now served as a carriage of nightmares drawn by primeval beasts. Usually accompanied by her mate, Homer, it was just Marge today. Slugger noticed her acting strange and resistant to his control over the reins.

Several gunshots echoed from the tail of the caravan. Slugger growled and signaled his men to pull over as he veered Marge off to the side. He rushed toward the source of the gunfire. "What's going on?" he demanded of the last car.

"There's a fucking Koopa tailin' us," the driver responded immediately.

"Hmm . . . hey, Java! Where you at?" Slugger inquired through the airwaves. Up ahead, a wrinkled man with unusually bushy grey eyebrows and a weak chin hopped out of the sidecar of his partner's motorbike. He came strolling toward Slugger, strapped with an ArmaLite AR-50 sniper rifle.

"What can I do for you, Boss?" the gentleman asked. Suddenly, a monstrous roar rippled through the trees.

"You up for some hunting?" Slugger asked, and the man replied with a slow smile.

The party got back on the move, now with a lone truck trailing behind them. It took another anxious hour before the stalking beast made an appearance. Java lay down in the back of the truck while it sped up to the rest of the vehicles. He watched the dragon galloping after them through his scope and waited patiently, absorbing the tremors of the ride.

"If I aim at nothing, then nothing is what I will hit . . . I am the great marksman, and I deny the holy word . . . disarm," the marksman whispered to himself and to his gun as he lined up the shot and released his bullet. These words gave him power and calm; they were an amalgamation of repurposed quotes from the old-world novelist, Kurt Vonnegut. The elongated bit of metal entered the creature's gaping mouth and flew through its insides before being caught by the inner layer of the shell. The marksman stayed his smile as the choking reptilian tumbled forward and slid in the dirt, twitching. Java then spanked the top of the vehicle twice, and the truck immediately pulled a U-turn to retrieve the carcass.

After two more days, Slugger brought his men to the end of the forest; beyond was a barren wasteland, with nothing but cracked earth, sand, and a vengeful wind. They rode with the sun, praying for the mercy of a passing bat to cast its shadow, until they finally arrived home.

Home was an expanding, byzantine, and intricate settlement built within a massive canyon. Dozens of men stood at every post, and an elaborate drawbridge crashed to the broken ground to allow the vehicles to enter. Hollowed skulls of various life-forms resting on the railheads of the front gate welcomed the men. Two of the gatekeepers unhooked Marge from the convertible and led her toward a flourishing oasis at the center of the settlement. She rapidly imbibed from the waters, accompanied by warthogs, bats, and a pair of colorful prehistoric birds that rested on a dead willow tree that stood out amongst the surrounding green. A balding man branded with tattoos on his beer gut and a chainsaw strapped to his back approached Slugger's vehicle with a smile.

"Jim, my man, when'd you get back?" Slugger beamed.

"Got back two days ago, perfect timing or what?" Jim responded. Slugger jumped out of his car to shake hands with his lieutenant.

"So, what'd you find?" The warlord rubbed his palms together in greedy anticipation. Jim's excitement dimmed.

"We followed them pretty far . . . but eventually lost 'em. Didn't want to spend too much time out there, but my best guess, they're probably somewhere along the coast," he informed Slugger.

Slugger nodded, his expression unreadable. "Where's the big guy?" he asked. Jim's eyebrows sunk, clearly perplexed.

"I thought he was with you."

Slugger was taken aback. "Hmm . . . strange, thought he'd miss me." Marge let out a moan that resonated throughout the canyon. Slugger rolled his eyes. "I gotta go see the beast master." He started to walk toward the kennel and stables.

"Uhh . . . Boss," Jim interrupted. "The stables are empty and . . . he's gone. I thought he was with you."

Slugger paused, glanced back at Jim, then continued walking away with the wails of his war beast echoing for all to hear. He rested in his dank, stale chambers and stared into the night with a blank face. His web of concerns eventually forced his left eye to faintly shutter.

Suddenly, his massive steel door was pounded on from the other side. He headed toward the door and lifted a latch on it that revealed a peephole underneath. Once he recognized his guest, he immediately unlocked the door and struggled to pull it open. After he finally dragged the entrance wide enough, he welcomed a giant with a widening grin. "Where've you been?" Slugger inquired.

Big Ben, his loyal mute bodyguard, remained still and silent. His black stringy bangs poured over his eyes, broken chains hung at his wrists, he wore no shirt—none ever seemed to fit—and a yellow and purple burn shone on his chest like glistening filth. Slugger looked downward and saw that the gargantuan man was dragging a beaten and bloodied hostage who seemed on the verge of losing his grip on consciousness.

"Well, hello Beast Master. Seems to me you got yourself into some trouble," Slugger hissed. "Bring him in." The giant dragged the man in by the arm as commanded, then threw him toward the center of the room before turning to secure the door. The battered soul coughed out blood and clearly lacked the strength to rise from the ground. "Tell me what happened, exactly how it happened. If you get one minor little detail wrong, he'll know, and I'll ask him very nicely to pop your nuts like grapes. Start, now," Slugger demanded with heat in his breath.

The man cleared his throat and began, "Your monster . . . wuh . . . was wild; he was banging on the cage and hollerin'. I thought I should give him sss . . . sss . . . some open space, and . . . I lost con . . . control."

"Where is he?" Slugger demanded. The man shook his head and dropped his gaze. Slugger rushed to grab the man's face and directed it back toward him. "Where is my fucking turtle?" he asked once more.

"He's gone. I lost him by the . . . the crack a few days ago. I'll take you where . . ." The man then collapsed and insisted on catching his breath. Slugger looked at him in disgust.

"Yes, you will. Ben, give him some water and something to eat and get ready yourself . . . we leave at daybreak." The giant grabbed the old beast master and dragged him away.

* * *

Slugger and Ben were packing up before the sun's glorious return, the caged beast master already strapped down to the back of a truck. Jim appeared, rubbing his eyes. "Looks like you've found everybody," he remarked.

"This sack of shit let Homer out, and now he's loose somewhere around the crack," Slugger informed Jim with salt in his words. Jim looked at the helpless old beast master and shook his head.

"Give me a minute and I'll be ready."

"No. I need you here. I'm taking Ben and maybe a few others, but you're in charge while I'm gone."

"Sir," Jim said, stern but respectful. Slugger looked at him. "You are always out, doing things that are beneath you: questioning trespassers, checking borders, dealing with fires . .

. this place needs you. Can't I go instead?" Jim pleaded.

"No. I'm gonna leave Marge here. I need you to watch her," Slugger answered. Jim lifted a curious brow and then let out a deep exhale as it sank, signaling his reluctant compliance.

"Sure Boss, no problem. I won't let her out." He was slightly confused and worried but knew better than to dig for answers. He was highly respected amongst their ranks as both the captain of convoy and compound and second in command of defense and logistics. Still, out of all the men, Slugger was the one who demanded and inspired the greatest amount of fear and love.

"Protect her from the men," he added before turning away. Jim considered his words before walking off toward the stables.

The gate suddenly wound down, and Slugger looked out to see who was approaching. A muddy buggy with relatively large wheels sped past the gate and drifted to a dramatic halt. Sand and dust blew into Slugger's—and the rest of the ground gate crew's—faces. Ben stood still, unfazed, while Slugger ground his teeth. The driver came out with a terrified young face. The boy, no older than thirteen, was blonde and blue-eyed and wore a backward hat.

"Slugger, I'm so sorry man, I . . . I didn't see you," the boy desperately pleaded. Slugger's vexation faded away.

"Billy, my boy. You got some skills behind the wheel," he said before approaching the boy and roughly patting him on the back. "How is everyone?" he asked genuinely.

"Everyone's good sir," the boy said. Willie exited the passenger side with excitement.

"Didn't think I'd see you so soon," Slugger stated, grateful to see him.

"You should have seen it; it was something special," said Willie with an unfamiliar expression in his eyes.

"What?" Slugger asked.

"Everything was burning . . . and then it started to rain. It was one, single cloud following the flames and putting them out, and then it just disappeared when it was done," Willie explained. Slugger remained silent, annoyed at this suspicious uncertainty.

". . . Homer's loose around the crack somewhere. Can you gather fifteen men and meet me at the closest post in two days?" he said, changing the subject.

"I can be there tomorrow," Willie stated with confidence.

"Good. Safe travels gents, we're gonna get an early start," Slugger called while climbing into the driver's seat of the truck. Big Ben, who was waiting patiently by the passenger side, entered the vehicle once his master had. They drove off, kicking dirt into Billy's face while Willie, anticipating this behavior from his commander, dodged the gust in time.

"Fuck's sake, I said I was sorry," Billy murmured while wiping his face clean. Willie laughed.

The trio sped through the desert with the heat bearing down upon them. They took a path east of the canyon, and it soon vanished with only barren wasteland and flat earth on all sides. The frail man in the cage was seemingly unconscious, while Slugger was overcome with a familiar paranoia. "You think it was a good idea to leave her behind?" he asked his companion. The leviathan, however, just remained silent and motionless. "Yeah, you're probably right. She'll be okay."

After a few hours, they saw a proud rock formation with a small wooden structure on its pinnacle in the distance. As they approached, Slugger began to wonder why they weren't being hailed. "Where the fuck are they?" he said to himself as he put the vehicle in park near the base of the rocks. A rope ladder attached to the structure swayed in the wind. Slugger irritably climbed to the top and found the outpost abandoned. He grabbed a water bottle and began to gulp it down without mercy, then threw another down to the others. Ben picked up the water and drank from it quietly before slamming the cage to wake up the beast master. He woke in fear, but seemed relieved to find he was being offered a drink.

Slugger picked up a leather and brass telescope and utilized it to scan the surrounding area but found nothing but scarred earth and rugged desolation. Unsettled, he climbed back down and went straight for the cage. "This is all on you. You took my Homer from me, but more importantly, you took him from Marge . . . and now she's gonna be whining and smacking her tail around until she dies because that's what these things do. I separated them, hoping it would make them stronger and break them of that behavior . . . but you can't break instinct. I fucked up and I realize that now, but what the fuck made you think you could just waltz in and take my animals out whenever you wanted?" Slugger asked. Despite the hoarse fire in his throat, his face was unreadable, expressionless.

The old man brought out a confused look. "Because I'm the beast master?" he eventually answered.

"That meant feed them, care for them . . . clean their fucking shit. I'm the fucking beast master, you're just the faggot I let call himself that." Creases cracked the warlord's face.

The night started to swell up and the bitter cold crept in. Slugger and Ben sat around a fire by the truck, both staring at the hypnotically sputtering flames. Through the dark, another light appeared. In the corner of his sight, far off, a pair of headlights blinked twice. Slugger immediately got up and rushed to the truck, then flashed his lights four times. Not a moment later, a pack of engines snarled to life and began moving closer. Another pickup truck and a fouled-up motorbike approached the fire while Slugger and Ben welcomed their arrivals.

Willie hopped out of the passenger seat, accompanied by nine other intimidating dragoons. "Always early, huh? You guys truly are some badass motherfuckers, rolling up here in the dead of night. Wasn't expectin' you 'til morning," Slugger praised them.

"Could only afford nine hands right now, but these are some of the toughest sons of bitches I've worked with. We'll get your beast," Willie said. "We also found something down south . . . something definitely worth investigating," he added.

"You find the fuckers who were supposed to be here?" Slugger inquired.

"Yeah, we found 'em . . . and buried what we could. Looked like Homer had his fun with 'em, but that's not what I want to show you," Willie explained.

* * *

They charged with the morning grey, leaving behind a storm of dust and sand. A prevailing wind seemed to ride against them defiantly. The party rode through a sea of nothing until something grew more apparent in the distance. Ahead was a great chasm that stretched out beyond sight; a deep gash within the planet that acted as a moat guarding a new land.

The warlord put his ear to the wind and faintly heard . . . a roar. As faint as it was, it still carried weight and induced fear. It was as if a living horn with teeth and hunger had blown, signaling from afar. For a moment, he thought it was his delusions toying with him yet again—and then he caught it once more.

"Stop!" he ordered. As the others screeched to a halt, Slugger attempted to discern where the sound had originated from. The echoes floated from beyond the crack. "It's this way!" Slugger barked and gestured for Ben to drive toward the source.

"Sir!" Willie bellowed from behind, but the pair ignored him and kept on. They arrived at the chasm yet heard nothing. Some of his men looked down with dread into the endless pit, a still and ravenous darkness.

"How'd he get over?" the concerned leader asked himself.

Willie approached him. "There's a crossing, jus' down south. We gotta hurry," he stated. Slugger nodded in response.

"But first, we gotta dump some baggage." The warlord looked with a grimace toward the caged beast master, who remained unconscious, and then over at Ben with a wink. The giant understood what he intended and unstrapped the cage from the back of the truck. He dragged it out with one arm.

When the cage crashed to the dirt, the beaten old man awoke and began crying hysterically. Ben then dragged the cage toward the edge of the crack. "Originally, I was going to feed you to Homer . . . thought for some poetic justice, but, looking down into this thing, I realize something now; I've never fed anyone to this." The sadist's smile widened.

"Please! Don't, I . . ." before the prisoner could utter his final pleas, Big Ben nudged the cage off the edge and the man's screams echoed into silence. The cage bounced back and forth against the walls until the darkness swallowed him and suppressed the sounds of the final impact.

After a little more than an hour, they arrived. At the sight of the crossing, the chieftain grew unsettled and irritated. An enormous steel pipe rested on the bottleneck of the crack where the two sides were relatively close, forming a bridge. The grand pipe was bolted down into the rock with chains laced into the sides for grip. "Who the fuck . . ."

Chapter III – A New Frontier

"Not sure who, but it was recent. Look . . . you can see tire tracks on the other side," Willie relayed to his commander.

"You think Homer was taken," stated Slugger. "We need more men," he then muttered under his breath.

"Sir . . . the tracks are relatively fresh, but we can't wait too long, or we'll lose 'em," Willie stated.

Slugger sunk his brows in a moment of contemplation. "Brody. Go back and grab twenty more men, but make sure Jim stays. Come to this point and wait for further instructions, understood?" he commanded. An olive-skinned gentleman with a wilting mohawk nodded before he mounted his bike and sped back toward headquarters. "If this is a reconnaissance mission, then we need to have a backup plan," Slugger announced.

The crew had no other choice but to abandon their vehicles and take only what was needed. They carefully crossed the thirty-foot pipe bridge, one by one. The last man to cross slipped off the bridge but was able to grab hold of the chains and pull himself back up. Once they were over, they looked in all directions and found nothing different, just the same barren landscape. "I can't see any tracks," Slugger complained.

"This way, hurry," Willie bellowed from up ahead. The men

journeyed through broken terrain and refused to surrender to an approaching sandstorm. Grains of sand sliced through cloth and flesh in an unrelenting gale. The time of day was uncertain, and the sky was seemingly lost forever. The group endured, digging their steps deep into the sand to not get taken away by the wind.

The storm seemed endless, but then the cascade of sharp grain suddenly ceased. The sand, like a harsh mist, washed away and revealed a hidden world. "Stop!" Willie warned his comrades. They were at the edge of a cliff looking down into an ocean of iridescent jungle blossoming from the corpse of an old town. The trail was cold, rinsed away early on by the storm. It was a hunch and a gamble that had led them here.

Slugger felt small in a growing world, but reined in his focus when he saw a far-off slope that gently led into the jungle below. It would take them off course to reach it, but seemed much safer than scaling down the cliff's edge.

Slugger pointed toward it, but Willie shook his head. "See how it curves around to meet that clearing? They have a vehicle, but we can cut them off if we head down this way."

"Alright then," said the warlord, nodding.

The group continued down the side of the treacherous cliff until they were deep in unfamiliar land. All managed to descend unharmed. The turf made the ground soft like thick and coarse carpet. Everything had been swallowed up by a high tide of green, including the wood and stone. The jungle was tight and dense with twisted trees tangled among broken buildings and abandoned sentiment.

They wandered aimlessly for hours in hopes of catching any signs of hunters or large beasts. Slugger sensed his men's fleeting energy and suggested a break. The sun hadn't fully vanished, but the dense canopy of the jungle kept the light at bay, and the little that did trickle in had a dreamy greenish glint. Once camp was set and the men began to rest, Willie took the opportunity to counsel his commander in chief. He took a seat next to him on a low sweeping branch.

"We need to hurry. We could lose the element of surprise any minute if we haven't already." Slugger ignored him and chose to stare off into the matted patterns of the flooring, where leaf, flower, root, and rubble alike were one with the undergrowth. ". . . Sir?" Willie growled.

"One more day and we'll head back," Slugger eventually let out, though he refused to break his gaze from where it was stuck in place. Suddenly, a terrible snore snapped at the air. The two glanced over toward Ben, who was fast asleep, sitting upright against the foundation of what used to be a fireplace, rhythmically failing silence for once. At his side gripped in his hand was a steel mace, forty inches long and with no spikes at the tip, just a perfect metal ball. The sight brought them both a moment of amusement.

"Why don't you rest for a bit. I'll keep watch," Willie suggested. Slugger gratefully nodded and left him to his post.

The night grew old, the atmosphere remained brash, and the world became still. While the men slept, Willie carefully worked on his wooden carving, shaving away imperfections with his blade. The carving resembled a reptile with a spiky shell and a long, elegant tail. It was a war turtle, same as Homer and Marge; it was a gift.

Eventually, a dim and blue glow in the distance caught his attention. He turned to face it, and the intensity increased in his mind once his eyes locked on it. It was an orb—tantalizing, perfect, and beautiful. Willie could not look away; he was hypnotically drawn to the spectacle. The sounds of the wilderness and slumbering men were replaced by a subtle humming. He slowly stood up and stared at the orb in the distance for ten minutes without blinking or moving.

Then, suddenly, he began walking toward the light's source. The knife and carving fell from his hands without concern. He tripped on some protruding roots and fell face-first into the earth. He lay there motionless for a few moments before getting back up. Dirt, twigs, and grass decorated his face, yet the man seemed unaffected. He started again toward the illumination, unfazed by brush or branch.

When he finally approached the floating orb, he kept himself from touching it. Eventually, with a predator's patience, the orb was sucked back up into a Jurassic pair of jaws that latched onto the ghost of a man from above. Willie did not struggle. The chomp tore through his flesh effortlessly, and his waist outside of the bite slid off the teeth and to the ground. The creature then swallowed the upper torso in one gulp. The narrow jaws belonged to a stationary beast; an organism rooted to the ground. The great carnivorous flower once again disguised its snout amongst its blood-red petals and reveled in its success.

The great star's rising brought about a panic and the stale scent of blood. The men frantically scattered in search of their lost comrade while Slugger, holding on to Willie's abandoned carving, tried to bury his anger and distress.

"We found something," a man relayed. His skin was burnt and leathery, and one eye was stuck in a permanent squint. He led Slugger to the predatory plant, which was protected by a ring of trees and green walls of thicket. Willie's icy bottom half lay on the ground. Slugger stared at the resting creature with bewilderment as its incisors glistened and oozed a green slime. “Shall we hack it down or burn it?” the man asked his commander.

“No, let’s move,” Slugger hesitantly relayed.

“Without Willie?” the man raised his voice.

“Can we do otherwise?” Slugger yelled back.

“We should go back,” the man suggested.

“Not . . . just . . . yet,” the warlord insisted with a twitch in his eye and drips of venom falling from his words.

They wandered aimlessly—again—while Slugger, lacking confidence, led his hunger-stricken crew into uncertainty. The jungle began to open up with fewer buildings and sparser trees. It felt spacious and free, but it was curiously quiet. When daylight died and the violet half-moon took its stage, the night revealed the hazy glow of a fire far off in the distance.

* * *

The fire was dim and half-heartedly surrounded by boulders and metal parts to cover the true extent of the flame. Huddled around it were four men, and resting to the side were three hunting dogs. The leader began to snap his finger and tap his foot rhythmically. “One, two, three . . . It’s been a haard day’s fight! And I’ve been workiiiin like a bosss.” The quartet began to sing in unison, following the beat. “It’s been a haard day’s fight, I should be sleepiiiin all night loong! But when I get sight of you, I find the—okay stop! Stop!” the leader interrupted. “Alex, you sound like shit.”

“What the fuck is that supposed to mean?” the man to his far left inquired.

“You’re not even trying man, don’t tell me you were,” the leader explained.

"I'm sick of this . . . I want to perform our shit! I want to sing my songs!" As he yelled, the dogs began to grow irritated. The leader looked over to them with dismay and then back to his companion.

"Don't start yelling. It doesn't matter what you want, we must give the people what they want . . . and they don't want something new, they want something old."

"Fuck that! Maybe if we surprise them, they wouldn't even notice; maybe they'd enjoy it and want more!" the other insisted.

"No! And I told you to keep your fucking voice down!" the leader snapped back.

"Why?"

"'Cuz you're working the dogs up!"

As they argued, another man on the far right started to walk off. "Hey! Where are you going?" the leader asked.

"Takin' a shit!" he responded nonchalantly.

The man wandered until he found a tranquil enough spot. He pulled his trousers down, squatted over the grass, and began to relieve himself. As he was defecating, the ground scuffled. Before he could react, a clammy palm smothered his face and pulled it back while the cold sting of steel slid across his throat. The indecent man fell back into his excrement while his blood escaped through the wound.

Back at the fire, the dogs became even more riled up, and the leader of the quartet eyed the animals with suspicion. "Shut up!" he ordered his disgruntled subordinate.

"Fuck you!" he fired back.

"Quiet!" the leader insisted once more, and was finally able to silence him with a solemn look.

The air seemed predatory; they all felt the same stalking

presence in the night. The remaining three slowly grabbed their weapons from off the floor and put out the flame. The hounds remained relentless and wild, yanking at their leashes, which were lassoed around a tree trunk.

"Rusty?" the leader asked the darkness. When no response came, he aimed his rifle toward a shadow and discharged. A scream in response sounded off the chaotic shoot-out that ensued. It seemed a thousand shots were fired in just under a second, and then smoke filled the battlefield.

"Who got hit?" Slugger yelled through the leftover carnage.

"It's Richie, Boss," a man answered as he rushed to his dying friend and attended to him with medical patience. The curly haired man on the ground shuddered and endured a series of spasms as he held his shattered clavicle. Slugger yanked out a rag tucked underneath his belt and gave it to the grieving flesh-stitcher, who used it to slow the blood flow.

"Get him up! We gotta take him back!" a regretful Slugger barked at his men. Suddenly, a comforting palm rested on his shoulder. It was the burnt man with leathered skin, and he was shaking his head forlornly. Slugger faced him. "Damn it!" the warlord roared in response. He shot a glance back toward the singers. Their dogs were piled up dead and the men themselves lay lifeless in their blood—all but one. The moonlight revealed a lone survivor slowly crawling away from the commotion.

"Not so fast." Slugger rushed his victim and kicked him to his back. The man had a goatee, trimmed and shaved, and eyes that were two separate shades of brown. His left hand was mostly blown off and his side had been grazed; a good chunk was taken out of his hip. Slugger searched into the man's soul until he noticed something spectacular on the ground beside him and picked it up. It was an antique hunting rifle, but the polished jaws of a war turtle were situated on the barrel of the weapon. The tip of the barrel poked out of the turtle's skeletal and permanent snarl.

"This . . . is . . ." Slugger awkwardly paused in momentary denial, ". . . incredible. Did you make this?" he inquired politely. The man remained silent. "Listen man, we weren't trying to kill you guys or take your stuff; we wanted more people to join our team. We watch a little bit as a vetting process, you understand?" The man nodded. "Good! This is probably no surprise to you, but this tends to happen quite often . . . the nature of this world and its inhabitants, right?"

"So, what happens now?" the injured man finally mustered up his speech.

"Well, we can save you, but I have to ask—and remember, this is for our own safety—why were you guys singing? It seemed like you were practicing for something." The man remained unsure and silent. "Alright then, we're going to go bury our fallen friend. Hopefully you won't bleed out by the time we come back, and maybe by then you'll have figured out an answer," Slugger hissed with charismatic darkness.

"We were practicing . . ."

"For?" nudged the warlord.

"There's a city," the man whispered while dropping his head and gaze—guilty, ashamed, and dying. Slugger turned around, intrigued.

"A city?"

"Yes," he replied reluctantly.

"How many people live in this city?"

"Thousands . . . maybe more," the man said, emboldened with a slight sense of pride. Some of Slugger's men muttered in the backdrop after hearing such a claim. Slugger's smile widened ear to ear, and a gap in his teeth revealed his missing molar.

"So, you guys are some kind of performers, eh? What's your name, friend?" The menacing interrogator began to wind down his inquiry.

"Alex Bolt."

"Well, Alex Bolt, where is this city? We would like to apply for residency," Slugger asked with eerie excitement.

"Please, help me." The man began to weakly flutter his hands as his vision became scarce and his skin grew cold.

"Someone fucking save this guy," snapped the warlord. The man attending to Richie's cold corpse ceased what he was doing and immediately rushed over. He examined Alex while rummaging through his sack of medical supplies.

"Can someone start a fire? We need to singe some flesh," the apocalyptic surgeon requested. The injured man fell out of consciousness, and Slugger picked up the decorated hunting rifle by the strap and hucked it around his shoulder. The jaws of Homer mounted on the gun looked up toward a black and blue sky, littered with white starry sparks.

The hours began to slip by, and the men erected a fire to cook the canines. Alex's wounds were wrapped up and his life force kept within him as he strayed further into unconsciousness.

The crew grew impatient by morning. "This is going to take forever," Slugger finally announced, then he stepped up to and slapped the man. The strike pulled his soul back into the realm of reality.

"Hey, hey . . . easy now." Slugger tried to ease the man's panic as he wiped drool from his hand. "I had to slap you because, well . . . we weren't sure you were gonna make it. My man Canada saved you; he learned how to be a goddamn flesh-stitching surgeon out here, all by himself. This is why we look for people. My men are irreplaceable and uniquely valuable. I couldn't ask for more from them, but I want more for them. We are wanderers in need of a home; can you take us to this city now? We are quite hungry."

"Uhh . . . yeah. North, just another day or two," said the man, unsure whether he should be grateful or suspicious.

"Do you or any of these dead gentlemen have a map of any kind?" Slugger asked.

"They might, but I know the way," he responded.

The gang searched through the supplies with little respect for the carcasses that lay between them. Eventually, someone found the map in the leader's back pocket. Slugger yanked it out of the man's hand and analyzed the impressive amount of detail. The area covered by the map seemed vast and even included the great crack and the newly installed pipe bridge. At the edge of the map, just past the bridge, was a blank yellow space labeled *"Unexplored."* This he knew was his area, his wasteland, his home. The thought of a bigger group coming into his lands angered him and filled him with an insecurity he thought he'd left behind. Then he found a red circle in the center labeled with the name: New Blake-Shire City.

Chapter IV – The Voice of Reason

Slugger approached one of his soldiers. The man towered over the warlord while the greenish sunlight flickered off his hairless cranium. "Go back with the rest of the men, meet with Brody, and bring the boys back here to this point. Me and Ben will meet you here in fourteen days," said the warlord. The henchman ground his fangs together. Slugger looked at him with sunken brows. "There an issue, buddy?" he asked with surfacing tension.

"We aren't coming back," the man responded. Slugger's smile twitched.

"You serious?"

"We'll go back, give them the map, and tell 'em how to get here, but we're heading home after that," said the grimacing man.

"Really? 'Cuz that's not what I just said." Slugger looked over at the stranger, then back at the mutineer.

"We've been out here too long. You got Richie killed, and you got Willie killed. And for what? A dumb animal? We're done with this shit. I'm not getting any more of my crew killed!" the man shouted.

"Arnold, my friend . . . it doesn't have to be like this," said Slugger as he inched closer to the man. Arnold drew his pistol, stepped up to his leader, and pressed the muzzle against his chest.

"I'll fucking kill you . . . you think I won't? I'm not scared of you or that fucking freak behind you. Out of respect for who you are and what you've done, I will relay that message, but I am going home afterward, and if you choose to get in my way, I will pump a hole through that cold empty fuckin' heart of yours."

Slugger dwelled on the man's fearsome gaze. ". . . No," he whispered to himself as he drew his right blade out and attempted to knock Arnold's aim off to the side with a quick swipe. He managed to push the gun off to the left, but Arnold was able to squeeze the trigger in time and discharge a blast through the tyrant's shoulder. At the same moment, Slugger's blade lodged into the other man's nose, tearing through the cartilage and through to the back of the skull. Slugger and the now lifeless Arnold fell to the ground as the others stood around and watched. Ben took a few steps toward them as Slugger shouted, "Canada! Canada, where the fuck are you?"

The surgeon rushed over and tended to his leader. "Looks like it went clean through," he relayed, hopeful while pressing the exit wound.

"Who else—ehh, fuck!" The pain of surgery interrupted Slugger's thoughts until he gathered himself and continued from the ground, "Who else shares the same attitude as our dear old friend Arnold?" The crowd remained obediently silent. "Now, he didn't die because he challenged me, no; he died because he threatened me. I mean, why do you guys think I'm in charge? Honestly? Because I'm the biggest and baddest? If that were the case this big scary fuck over here would be in charge . . . or his brother would still be," the warlord explained.

He was gazing at Ben, who lacked any cognitive response.

"I'm in charge because I'm the smartest and the maddest, and those two qualities have gotten us pretty fuckin' far in the apocalypse. In the end, I know I am nothing without you all . . . but everything we have, everything we've got, who and where we are in this world, is because of me. I know what I'm doing and frankly, by now, you should all already know that."

The crew dug two graves and laid there fallen friends into the earth while Canada remained by Slugger's side to further analyze the wound. Ben kept a watchful eye on Alex as instructed, and the proceeding day and night were followed by rest and gathering up their strength.

"You need at least a week to rest. You're lucky, but don't be a dumbass. You should go back with us; we can come back for this place when you're ready," said the surgeon.

"I am ready. Now patch me up, we move out in a few hours," Slugger stated confidently while giving his friend a playful slap to the face. The groups split without any farewells or reassessing of the plan, leaving the warlord and his enforcer alone to carry on, guided by a stranger.

Hours later, Slugger and Ben crafted a makeshift sled with bedding out of branches, leaves, rope, and cloth, and the giant dragged their incapacitated guest. They exited the mangled forest grove and welcomed the retreating sun from atop a ridge that looked out even farther than the first. In the distance, they could make out a farm surrounded by massive stumps that resembled tombstones in a graveyard. The land was cultivated and tamed, and a small group of men catered to the operations, clearly shutting down for the coming night.

Near the farm were two vast pens separated by an aging farmhouse. Grazing cattle and tusked hogs were cramped securely in one while the other seemed to encompass thick, black, writhing logs. They looked like giant caterpillars of some sort, and seemed to be feasting on a field of foxfire fungi that started to glow as dusk deepened. Patches of rose-colored fuzz sprouted randomly all over the creatures' bodies. The dim lights housed inside the fuzz were flies symbiotically linked to the squirming herd, and they never strayed far. The flies' wings were blue at rest and glowed within the thin rose fuzz, but shimmered white in flight.

Behind the farmhouse was a nearly hidden orchard that twinkled in the shade like the very stars it was under. Off to the side of that orchard was a lonely red barn, and a windmill sat a bit farther away from the barn on a small rounded hill.

Slugger could make out all these details from where he stood. It seemed to him that the cracks above the windows made the barn look angry, like it had an old and twisted face. He admired the facility, and was enticed. The giant set the sled down, giving Alex a view at the edge.

"Those guys will fix us up some supper, and then we'll be at the city by midday," he insisted, though his face looked ripe with internal doubt.

Slugger turned to face him. "I am sorry for what you witnessed. I'm sure it paints a nasty picture of me. Hierarchy is easier to establish than to maintain. I'm sure your people can understand that, especially at your scale?" he inquired.

"How many of you are there?" Alex finally asked, as if the question had been sitting at the back of his head for too long, ready to burst. Slugger stared back with a blank face but said nothing. Alex saw the war turtle skull peek out from behind him. He'd noticed how Slugger always kept it close, not like a weapon, but rather a sentimental treasure, and then he recalled the way the madman had first looked at it. "What was with the dumb animal comment . . . you some kind of monster enthusiast?" he asked, hoping to relate.

"I am," Slugger answered bluntly while glancing back to admire the decorated rifle yet again.

"Same . . . back at New Blake-Shire, we're kinda famous, you know. We'd go out to find all types, no matter how big and scary. They called us poachers. We've seen just about every beast out here," Alex said proudly, though he failed to hide the fear that sang behind his words and crawled up his skin. It was shaky, his voice, but turned loud and forced whenever he noticed it trailing too weak. "We—"

"Tell me the story of how you got this set of jaws," the warlord said, his eyes latched on the ivory fangs.

Alex cleared his throat. "Umm . . . yeah, well, we heard it from far away. Blaring and blasting and smacking his tail. Once we found him . . ." he began, staring off in reminiscence, almost forgetting himself, "we filled him with tranqs. The ones that didn't bounce off his shell got him in the face, neck, eye . . . down his fucking throat, and he didn't even flinch. We kept filling him up until finally, he dropped. Then we filled him up with more, just in case. We wanted him . . . I wanted him, like no other. He was a dinosaur, a dragon, with blood and fire in his eyes." Slugger stared at him, listening. "Then he woke up, or had some kind of postmortem spasm, thrashing and spitting until he knocked the tow down a steep cliff, almost taking us with him."

"The fall killed him?" asked the warlord through the pain lodged in his throat.

"Yeah . . . but I was able to take his head and make that," Alex said, smiling nervously.

Slugger looked at the rifle. The bone was clean and pale, with very few cracks. The jaws were now stuck forever snarling. He looked at it longingly. Homer, Marge's mate, was no more, and what killed the warlord the most was how he had died; not with his lover or in his home, but picked clean by these buzzards. To all those who dwelled in the canyon, Homer was a king.

"I . . . what about the bridge?" he asked.

Alex paled, knowing exactly what he was referring to. His fears were confirmed; he and the other poachers had led this group here. "We put it there, a week before. The beast was gnawing at it but seemed too scared to cross."

"It looked quite permanent," suggested Slugger. "Planning on makin' regular visits?"

"Part of our job is exploration and discovery. What's it matter to you?"

The warlord scoffed. "Where's the body?"

"Gone," Alex insisted.

"What do you mean?" snapped the warlord.

"It fell into an asphalt lake."

"What?"

"A tar pit," Alex explained, "along with the truck. There's no way to get them out now. We were able to grab what we could, but trust me, you do not want to slip into that shit."

Slugger eventually contained himself, and a deep exhale vented out his inner torture. "Thank you," the warlord muttered with genuine appreciation. He then took a few steps closer to the man. The singer's faux smile faded as he tried to see through the warlord's mask. "But . . . I don't . . . I don't need you . . . anymore." Slugger's words were thoughtful, trotted out with brief pauses. Alex could not break eye contact with his blackened and drilling gaze, and he suddenly felt frozen.

The crazed lunatic then proceeded to pounce on the man and smother his breathing, denying him the essential wind of life. The struggle lasted several agonizing moments while Ben remained like stone. The sled bent and cracked while the two entangled themselves in the cloth and leaves amidst the struggle. The dying man's eyes wandered, and then his strength diminished. Slugger stood over his latest victim triumphantly, cradling his injured arm and biting down the pain. "I'll do all the talking," the menace relayed to his monstrous guard.

* * *

"Sir! We got something up ahead. Two men, and one of 'em is pretty big . . . they're dragging a corpse and waving a white T-shirt like a flag." An armed gunman updated his commanding officer. The leader remained silent while he twisted his winding mustache.

"I will talk to them . . . keep your aim steady, be aware, and do not show yourself until necessary." The commanding officer was elderly, yet he still retained black in his hair. He wielded an authoritative South American accent and a stoic sense of wisdom. The sniper disappeared while another man escorted the smug madman and his brutal enforcer to the porch of the man in charge.

"Hello. My name is—" Slugger began.

"Why do you have a body?" the older man demanded while remaining comfortably seated.

"Well, I was going to get to that. I just wanted to tell you who we are. And what is your name, sir?"

"I tell you nothing, you ask me nothing. Now, why do you

have a body? Are you a salesman of some sort?" the head of the ranch insisted. Slugger's smile contorted upward.

"We came across four men . . . singing, I might add. We wanted to talk. We hadn't seen a friendly face in quite a while. We approached them and they fired. We lost our third compatriot and I got shot myself, but we killed them all." Slugger resorted to his blankness; his poker face. The elderly man in charge scratched his chin while Slugger continued, "All except this one, Alex Bolt I believe his name was."

The old man leaned forward to examine the corpse. The face seemed pulped and was beginning to blue; it was hard to recognize at first glance. "We tried to save him, but he took some bullets. We kept him alive for about a day or two . . . he told us to come here. He said he was sorry, and I said I was sorry, and then he died, right on that ridge up there. We aren't expecting food or supplies, but people—strangers—are a big deal these days. In the end I trusted him, and he saw we both wanted the same thing: to be with people again. It was just a chance. It always is, right?" The secret tyrant lifted his brows in an appeal to the man's humanity.

The old farmer pulled out a wooden pipe from his jacket's inner pocket. He then proceeded to pack a pinch of tobacco and topped it with a pinch of marijuana. Afterward, he began to rock in his chair while sparking and puffing away. Slugger began to doubt his master plan.

"So, you are a salesman. I bet you thought that story up on your way down here . . . it's a good story, I almost want to believe it. Does this one talk or, is he just your bodyguard?" He pointed with his pipe toward the giant mute.

"Not sure. He understands though," Slugger insisted with beads of sweat forming at his temples.

"Do you understand what I'm saying?" the man pressed.

Slugger responded with a fault in his mask. "Quite frankly, no. I don't know what you're saying."

"I'm saying you are a liar and a con artist. I can smell it; I can see it," the man continued.

"So . . . I'm guessing you haven't killed us yet because you think we might have some hidden numbers?" Slugger asked.

"I know you don't have any nearby numbers. My men surveying the area would have alerted me by now." The old man nudged a radio by his feet. "Don't try to scare me, gringo; I have protected this farm from far worse," he said.

"I'm sure you have. This world is full of things that are far worse than us . . ." said Slugger.

"Take 'em to the barn," the farmer commanded as he continued to puff on his nightly ritual. At gunpoint, they were led away. As they approached the barn, the warlord looked over toward his brutish friend and winked to ensure confidence in his leadership, however, his façade had started to crumble from within.

When the farmer finished his smoke, he closed his eyes and took in a deep breath. Eventually, he reached for his radio and tuned it to the proper channel. The sound of ruffled static penetrated the momentary peace. "This is the farmer . . . Huntress, are you out and about? Over," he broadcasted over the waves. The airwaves stayed clear, but he persisted. "I repeat. This is the farmer. . . Huntress . . . are you in the proximity? Over."

Finally, the twisting snap and crackle of the radio emerged with a response. "I hear you loud and clear, old man . . . what can I do for you?" The voice speaking the words resembled the sound of rain on steel.

"This time, I got something for you."

Chapter V – The Huntress

A woman wielding a blackened steel pike waded through the murky stream. She wore a thin hooded scarf with gaping tears along with a pair of kneepads and elbow pads, all scuffed to no end. Her face was sunken and cool, and she bore a gash where her left ear once was. She thrust her spear into the water then pulled it out, a creature impaled on the end. The stingray whirled its twin tails around frantically and writhed its elongated body. The spots on its slimy skin quickly cycled through a strange color palette. The Huntress watched the animal struggle at the end of her weapon until it slowed and finally ceased. The spots darkened to a red like blood, then faded to pink and finally a pale white that resembled pearls against its sleek black leather.

"They draw near!" a robotic voice alerted her from above. She tossed her catch into her satchel and rushed up a flight of fading steps built into an abandoned river dam. Her surroundings were lush and green, but a stone bridge atop the dam had been maintained, as it was infrastructure still relevant to the survivors of the apocalypse.

When she reached the bridge, she was met by her companion, a warrior not of this world encased in a mechanized battle suit of metal. The bipedal machine stood close to the height of two men, had limbs capable of a wide reach, and carried a mounted shoulder turret. The creature's face was revealed behind a bubble of a helmet. His eyes were black, and his skin was a dark grey. Though its humanoid body filled out most of the inside of the armor, the creature's cranium mostly resembled an octopus's with an oval, sack-like skull. Tentacled arms extended from his lips and controlled a secondary focus cannon built into the upper cataphract.

"What do we got?" she asked the extraterrestrial.

"Twenty-four individuals, three carts, and a large cattle beast," he responded through a digital voice modulator.

"Cattle beast?" Curious, she used a pair of binoculars that were strapped to her neck to scout ahead. She cracked a smirk at the sight. "You mean an elephant."

"Elephant." The alien repeated the word in an effort to practice his speech. He had trouble speaking with humans. Their languages required much internal motion and effort and strained his temporalis- and caninus-type muscle structures. Still, the voice modulator technology allowed even a broken dialogue to sing clear.

The group of traders approached the Huntress and her off-world companion. A plump and rosy leader helmed the welcome with squinting excitement. "We are very much pleased to see you both; we have been without an escort for days."

The Huntress lifted a questioning brow. "Come on then, let's get settled," she said. The Vagantem warrior subtly admired the elephant, who was exquisitely covered in ceremonial paint and graffiti art. The beast of burden was transporting a myriad of food and supplies in baskets and sacks strapped to its medieval saddle. A woman riding atop the creature and wearing foreign jewelry and feathers that vibrantly shimmered in the sun smiled and winked coyly at the onlooker. "Ceteris," the Huntress said, attempting to reel in her friend's attention.

Nightfall cast its great shadow and claimed half the world while the caravan set up camp. Drinks and laughter taunted the wilds: civilization was on its crawl back. A thin man who compulsively stroked his beard into a sharp point drew closer to inspect his new protectors. "I gotta know . . . how did you and E.T. end up becoming so close?" he asked.

The Huntress smirked at the memory. "It's not really anything that interesting. I was a thief . . . I used to steal from caravans like this all the time. Until one day, they got smart. One huge-ass cart covered in sheets and shrouded in mystery came my way, and with only two men to guard it. Easy pickings, right?" Her grin grew wider. The rest of the camp was not amused, with the exception of the man with the pointed beard.

"I killed one man, and the other ran away. I lifted the covers to see my prize and next thing you know . . . I get electrocuted and I'm done, passed out. I woke up hogtied and getting dragged away. I'd never seen an alien up close before . . . I saw one on TV, I think, a while back, but he scared the shit out of me." She laughed. "He told me the trip home was going to be long, so if I wanted to talk, I could. But it was him who wouldn't shut up. He spoke of a city where Vagantem and people worked together, a place where I did not have to steal or talk to myself . . . a place we could both call home. He's been a loyal friend ever since," she said, passing off a sisterly nod toward the off-worlder.

"*Wunderbar*!" a gaunt fellow with the fresh blood of the German folk insisted. "Tales tell all. *Da steppt der Bär*!" he continued, though it quickly became apparent to him that the others could not understand him.

"... *Bär*," Ceteris repeated, and the voice modulator somehow portrayed his struggle while at the same time annunciating the word clearly. The Huntress could not refrain from giggling.

"What does that mean?" she asked.

"Well, that this is going to be a good party, of course," he replied with a fat man's smile, ironic on a man of his build. She smiled back.

"Excuse me, miss? What time shall we be expecting our departure?" asked a nearby trader before pulling his stick back out from the fire. Affixed at the point was a scorched critter, pulped and discolored, resembling a faceless, amorphous smoking piece of flesh. The question had been on the others' minds as well, and when it was finally asked, the crowd tuned in.

The Huntress sobered upon feeling all the eyes upon her. "We're not headed to the city; not yet at least," she said. The group grew eerily silent while the cooking flame continued to converse with the wooden fuel. The man who had asked dropped his food, and the one with the pointed beard shot her a look of disdain and disappointment while anxiously racing his fingers through oiled locks. The plump headman grimaced and turned away. All grew irritable at the idea of finally having the comfort of an armed escort, only to be shooed off. All but the German, who seemed even more jolly.

"My dear lady *kriegerin,* I have enjoyed the company of these fine people, but I will be parting from them as well. I will be here at the bridge a few more days conducting tests, you see. I am to draw a report on its structural integrity and overall current state. May I enjoy you and your friend's company until then?" he asked, halfway expecting his desired reply.

"Unless you got an offer to beat the farmer . . . that's where I'm headed," the Huntress stated, and the matter was put to rest.

By early morning, the jungle air was humid and heavy. The caravaneers awoke damp like leaves in the morning dew, and without their escorts. By midday, they were off to the city—all but one. The German wandered over to a bicycle, dull and black with mud caked around the spokes and bars. Attached to the back was a small camper meant for one, with a single solar panel on top. Inside, a short mattress consumed the floor, and along the walls were shelves with basic toiletries, cooking items, and measuring tools. A flickering light hung from the low ceiling along with a beaded chain. The man took out a toolbox and a notepad with a pen sheathed in the spiral binding.

* * *

As the Huntress and her space warrior approached their destination, she pulled out a walkie-talkie from within her pack. The thing was old, and it creaked as she tuned it. The static was soft, surprisingly. "This is Huntress and Ceteris. We are incoming . . . warning to your snipers, over."

"Farmer's waitin' for you at the porch . . . over," a voice shrilled through the radio. She did not respond and continued down the trail until it met a luxurious orchard fenced off with wrought iron. She waited in silence with Ceteris. Finally, a farmhand rushed to the gate to let them in. "Sorry, thought you were coming from the other side for some reason," the farmhand stated in his shrill voice. The Huntress remained stern.

"The other side," Ceteris muttered as they stepped through.

The fruit trees of the orchard were not strange to the two guests; not the misshapen apple or orange trees, not the leafless sticks spilling sap and covered in purple bulbs, not even the giant mushrooms that drooped strings from their canopies like jellyfish. They were led past the pens of cow and swine and fungi-feasting cattleworms to the porch where the farmer sat and smoked. He did not get up from his rocking chair but welcomed her with an ear-to-ear smile. "Señorita, how are you?" he asked.

"Señorita . . ." Ceteris muttered.

She smiled back, struggling to hold her stern mask. "How's it, Huego?"

"Well, it has been mostly quiet. We've missed you stopping by from time to time."

"I am all over the place now. People seem to know my name throughout the city. They make up stories about me . . . stories I kinda like and don't wanna bury. It's been so crazy lately, I'm actually starting to turn down work. You're lucky I didn't turn you down," she said playfully.

"Ahh, but this time is different, remember? I have something for you." He puffed gluttonously on his pipe.

The Huntress's warm smile remained, but turned hungry, almost sinister. "And what would that be?"

"I have a fighter . . . and a talker."

"Why do I need the talker?" she asked.

"Because . . . he has some strange control over the other. The fighter is a monster; almost the size of Ceteris here. I almost killed him on the spot; too dangerous to leave something like that roaming around. Then I thought, he would make a nice gift . . . could be the next big star."

"Hmm . . . you know, I'm becoming quite the star myself,"

she said.

"In the ring?" he asked, his brows furrowing.

"I don't fight other men anymore. I go straight to the Bowl."

"The Bowl? Señorita, you cannot be serious. Only the most foolhardy, the most stupidly unaware, or the ones who have a death wish step in there. Why do you do this to my heart?" He grabbed her hand with both of his and held it like a father would. "You are doing very well for yourself, is that not enough?"

"Enough," Ceteris repeated.

She nudged him softly against the cheek with her knuckle. "Don't worry 'bout me old man." Huego remained quiet, in thought. "Now, why don't you show me this fighter?"

"Don't forget the talker; they might be a package deal if I'm to understand it. Could make it easier for you. They're locked up in the barn, come around," he said as he lifted himself from his chair with much effort. Ceteris followed, but remained a short distance back in quiet thought. They approached the barn, sturdy as a castle and wise as a tree. "I did not like their look . . . still don't. But maybe a woman can render them more revealing," he said softly.

"Ahhh . . . you want me to interrogate them, is that it?" she said, understanding the farmer's motive.

"I want you to make your coin, and I hope these two bring you fortune and further fame. But . . . strangers from afar, bringing corpses with them and apologizing for killing our people? It is very strange, no?" His voice became grave and wary.

"What corpses?"

"The damned poachers are dead; they brought Alex Bolt's corpse back with them."

"Did you examine the body?" she asked.

"Maybe, why?"

"And . . . ?"

"And what? He was shot and near bloodless . . . I guess he did look a little beat up, but I assumed that was from dragging him along from God-knows-where."

"Why did they only bring him back?" The Huntress asked with unseeing eyes.

"They crossed paths and shots were fired before words. I guess Alex was still breathing, and he told them about Blake-Shire." The Huntress looked angered at this, but it flashed away, and her stern mask was put on once again.

"Have you gone and checked the site of the shootout?" she asked.

"We checked the ridge where he said he came from, where Alex might have died. The talker said he was unsure exactly where the firefight happened, so he's no help. I felt if I sent my men farther out, they'd stumble on a trap."

"What do they want?" Her eyes narrowed on his.

"To be with people, apparently," the farmer scoffed, unbelieving.

"Hm. Let me talk to them, are they restrained?" Huego only smiled and nodded. He then extended his hand toward the barn, signaling her to enter alone.

The door slid open, wailing like a wooden widow. The Huntress entered and shut it behind her. A man walked about the second story of the barn with a Dragunov sniper rifle, his trigger finger trembling. Cast with shade from the bill of his hat, his face was hidden until his eyes met hers for a moment.

Slugger and Ben were tied up, backs to each other and sitting on a bale of hay. Slugger faced the door and welcomed the Huntress with an off-putting smile.

"Hello there," he greeted, but she ignored him and strolled around to meet the other face. As she looked upon Big Ben, the fighter she was promised, she could not help but to put on a cold smile.

"You are a monster if I've ever seen one." The giant did not respond, and he let his bangs hang over his eyes. He barely moved, but the broken chains at his wrists still swayed and hissed. The Huntress was intrigued.

"You're better off conversing with me . . ." Slugger said. She walked over to face the talker.

"You speak for him?" she asked.

"Sometimes, but it's a lot more than that." The warlord's smile was dry and cracked; he smelled and looked hungry.

"What do you mean?"

"We are an inseparable pair . . . looking after each other since almost the start. He only speaks and listens to me. I trust him . . . and he trusts my lead," he said.

"Farmer's right . . . you are strange," she said, almost friendly.

"What else did the farmer say?" asked Slugger.

"He told me your story."

"Well, maybe you can tell me why he's so suspicious then?"

"Why do you think?" the Huntress asked with a smirk. Slugger had no answer. "Why are you here?" Her voice hardened and she inched closer, the cold smile fading away. Slugger still had no answer. She looked him in the eyes and did not look away for some time, reading his thoughts, sketching his face in her mind. Finally, Slugger spoke.

"What exactly are you so scared of?"

"Scared? Well . . . the weak link, of course, the chink in the armor. One troublemaker is all it takes. We've had many set-backs over the years, and with blood already spilled–especially from such names as renowned as the poachers—there will be much talk and many questions, and not just from the people."

Slugger could not work out what she had meant by that, and it seemed an hour to him before she spoke again. "What do you know of the Vagantem?" she asked, but Slugger did not reply. He began to feel like he was shrinking, and the world was no longer his.

"The Vagantem . . . the visitors, aliens from beyond the stars," the Huntress explained. "You do remember them, right?" she asked.

"They're back?" Slugger asked plainly, yet there was a shaky edge in his eyes.

"They never left," she said. Slugger's gaze fell and remained unfocused. He no longer was thinking of his plan, of Ben and his men, of the Lost Boys, or of the canyon; nor was he thinking of Marge or of Homer.

"Is something wrong?" she asked with a twisted smile. Slugger darted his eyes back to her. There was much he wanted to say, but couldn't articulate.

"Looks like you might need to mull a few things over . . ." the Huntress said as she turned to exit without looking back. Dying light momentarily shone in but was quickly blocked again by the shutting of the barn door.

Ceteris waited outside the barn, alone. His now greying eyes stuck to the Huntress as she walked past him and looked off into the distance as if there was an answer to be found in the evening air. He said nothing until she did. "Do you think I can ask you a favor?"

"Favor," he repeated.

"Yes. Can you go to that ridge up there and see if you can track their steps back to the kill site?"

"Yes, Huntress. I will see what I can find but . . ." he paused, thinking of the human words, ". . . we must return." She only nodded in response, then watched him vanish into nightfall. His heavy steps silenced eventually, along with the constant motions and mechanics within his suit that whistled, hummed, steamed, and clicked.

Back at the porch, Huego rocked in his chair with shut eyes, caught in a cloud of smoke. "I sent Ceteris to go check out the site. I'm gonna stay close to the barn, watch them through the cracks, see if I can . . . read anything," said the Huntress. Huego did not open his eyes, and he puffed further on his pipe.

"What did you find out?" he asked.

"Nothing new. Seemed to scare when I mentioned that the Vagantem were still around; should have brought in Ceteris. I have a hunch, but it's no confirmation," said the Huntress.

Huego opened his eyes and smiled. "What is this hunch?"

"Honestly, I think you are right. I think they tried to kill and steal from our people; and that coward, Alex, thought they would spare him if he sold us out."

Huego's smile faded. "What else?"

"They're after something. They're plotting something, or at least he is."

"You weren't in there for long," he mentioned. "What do you know that I don't?"

"Probably a lot," she said with a smirk.

"Maybe . . . but this, I already knew," he said impatiently.

The Huntress laughed, not outright disrespectfully, but with a sharp glassy prick to it. "Huego . . . I'm taking them to Blake-Shire anyway. I don't like strangers finding us before we find them any more than you do, but it does happen. The poachers were idiots . . . they probably sang into the night and let their fires burn. And Alex—" she scoffed, "what a little bitch. When Ceteris comes back and tells us what he found, we'll get a better idea of these two. Most likely they're just some random bandits trying to make a score.

"I should also mention, that if I end up losing them or having to kill them, then you will not only pay me for my time and travels, but also what I might have earned if I took another job. Fuck, I could have stayed back and protected some dude measuring a bridge. And now you're giving me shit for coming to pick up what I rightfully assumed was a gift?" She laughed again, bitterly. The farmer puffed and flicked his wrist angrily to shoo her away, cutting into his cloud. She shook her head with a smile and left.

Chapter VI – Borrowed Time

Ceteris returned the following night, when all at the farm were sleeping except for one restless sniper, who allowed the metal warrior to pass through his scope. The Huntress was also awake and waiting for him by the barn. "What'd you find?" she asked with that same hungry look Ceteris had expected.

"Blood . . . and death," Ceteris replied.

She looked at him, unquenched. "Are you sure that's all there was?" He locked with her gaze and said nothing so she would read his eyes instead. This tactic was usually convincing enough, especially after all the two had been through. "Were there any signs of a big party? How many do you think—"

"No more than three or four . . . along with the poachers," said the alien solemnly.

"So, he was telling the truth?" she asked, unsure.

"The truth . . . I believe so." Ceteris's voice was strong and mechanical. She nodded vacantly.

"Let's get some rest," said the Huntress as she patted the Vagantem on his bulky metal back. For a moment, she thought she felt a piece missing, a gap or indent that was not previously there; still, her suspicion was unaroused.

* * *

The sky was black and blue and purple as the sun readied to peek out from behind the world. A strange bird squawked as if to prepare the land for the coming day. Two farmhands led the cows and swine outside; at the end of their pen was a rickety shed that housed the animals at night. The cattleworms from the opposite pen, however, were always left out. If the sun was too harsh or the rain too heavy, there was a metal awning that slid out along rusted rails over the majority of their pen. The operations picked up, and Huego exited the farmhouse, twisting his mustache.

"I don't suppose you have a vehicle I can borrow?" the Huntress asked, sitting at the porch in the old man's rocking chair. Huego smiled.

"For you, señorita . . . anything."

They were given a truck. It was missing the right-side door and all the windows but the windshield had been broken through. The bed was full of hay and one of the wheels was deflated. Ceteris was already waiting outside the barn as she pulled up. "Keep your guns on 'em, the whole ride there," she said.

She threw open the door to the barn and the early light blasted inside. "You gonna help me?" The Huntress eyed the sniper, and he knew what she wanted. He took aim at the prisoners and directed them outside. Slugger and Ben, blinded by the light, struggled to get up, as they were still attached at the back by rope. When the giant made it to his feet, he unknowingly lifted Slugger in the air. The warlord felt humiliated as his cold, bootless feet dangled like a child's. He still smiled, despite it all, though his face was drawn with veins and his eye had started to twitch. As Ben exited the barn, Slugger watched the guard smirk and snicker at him. His anger soon flushed away when he saw Ceteris.

The Vagantem towered over them; even Ben had to look up to see his face. Despite the presence of the otherworldly being, Ben had no reaction. No sound of wonder, no jump of fear; not even the breath leaving and entering his body changed.

Ceteris stared back, looking through Ben's wiry bangs curiously. He then made his way around the giant to meet the mouthpiece. His steps thundered, and Slugger's eyes widened and goosebumps raised his skin as he came face to face with the creature. Never had he seen one of them before; part of him had wanted to believe they were a lie, a myth made to cover government failures. But they weren't a lie; in metal and flesh, here one stood. Slugger had no words. The Huntress smiled deviously, watching the silent interaction. "Can you put 'em in the back?" she then asked.

Metal hands extended from the bulky wrists, as if they were another set of tools cycled out. Ceteris hoisted them both up by the rope. Slugger heaved, but Ben remained quiet, audibly unaffected. The power exerted strained the mechanized suit. Clicks, steam pressure, and whistles grew louder until the two were dropped roughly in the bed of the truck. The truck sunk and squealed. Ben followed Slugger's lead as they propped themselves back up onto another hay bale seat.

The warlord had had enough. "Who in the fuck do you people think you are?" he asked bitterly, and it seemed white, molten steel fell from his mouth and scorched the earth, but it was just hot, foamed spit.

The Huntress giggled. "I've been there before . . . be cool, you'll be fine." Slugger eyed her, then looked back at the massive cosmic foreigner. Too many paranoid thoughts ran through his mind. He was uneasy, more than usual. The captive warlord then shut his eyes and started to breathe slowly, trying to meditate. Think; he had to think his way out.

* * *

Huego watched them drive down a green road just beyond the orchard, through a tunnel of flowers. He then reached for his pipe.

The ride was bumpy, and the truck seemed to limp with its deflating tire. The Huntress drove while Ceteris strode behind them, sending tremors with each step. His eyes stayed on Ben's, as the silent giant was faced back. They were going slow, in part due to the state of the vehicle and in part due to the coarse path. Small rocks blended with the greenery, acting as natural speed barriers and adding another annoyance for the warlord to stew over.

No one spoke or made a noise other than the mechanical intricacies of the alien power armor. It seemed to eventually blend in with the singing of birds and insects and trees. Slugger was tired, hungry, and sore, and he could only assume Ben was in the same shape. Finally, he lifted the silence and spoke through a paneless back window while meeting the woman's eyes in the rearview mirror.

"You and the Mexican seem to be going pretty far out of your way on account of us . . . don't you think?" As he asked, he looked around and noticed the flowery tunnel was thinning into walls of sparsely green thicket.

"How do you know he's Mexican?" the Huntress asked.

"Is he?" She shrugged at the question, unsure herself. "So, you gonna fuckin' level with us yet?" Hot froth foamed from his lips.

She looked at him coolly for a moment, then the ends of her lips twisted upward. "People . . . you want to be with people again, no?"

Her smugness irritated him, the fact that he was a prisoner sickened him, but the idea his plan had failed . . . the very notion that he had so cockily walked up and given up his position of power nearly killed him inside. "This is your way of bringing in new people?" he asked.

"Depends on the nature of the encounter. Doesn't that seem fair?" Her words were taunting yet again. He had no response to this. Then he caught a glance under her scarf hood as he leaned over.

"Jesus Christ . . . what the hell happened to you?" Slugger quickly realized how callous that might have seemed and turned his head to make sure the alien wasn't sneaking up on him, but there he was, roughly fifteen feet back, keeping up and staring at him with cosmically black eyes. They seemed to change color for no particular reason from grey to black, but this time, they were speckled with grey and white stars. The sight sent a chill up Slugger's bones that he tried to forget.

The Huntress's cruel smile did not fade after the question, or the tone. She looked at him, almost like looking down at a lowly creature. This angered him more. "What does it look like? It got bitten off."

"By what?" This time, he was more curious than spiteful.

"I don't even know if we have a name for it."

"Tell me what it looked like," he almost demanded, forgetting himself, but she only smiled ever more wickedly.

"Like a cross between a lion and a wolf except it had hind legs like a frog's or rabbit's. The mane was purple against grey and blue fur, and it had a short tail like a bunch of bristles. By far the loveliest thing I have ever seen . . . and the most fierce," the Huntress said with a giggle at the end.

Slugger suddenly calmed and he could not understand why. He looked at her, desperately curious. "Never seen one of those before," he confessed.

"No one has, apparently. No one believes me when I explain it . . . and the few Vagantem who speak English don't seem very interested in these creatures, and they outright refuse to tell you anything about what exactly happened all those years ago and why . . . not even Ceteris." Slugger noticed the frustration, though she kept it subtle. He hated these things more and more; every time he heard their name, and every time he looked upon the hulking alien warrior.

The Huntress, however, did not hate the Vagantem, despite the deepening frustration she had with them. This, Slugger could almost read. "Why are they still here?" he asked, spitting fire.

"They're stranded . . . they have no world to go back to." The Huntress was not concerned with this fact.

"So, they came and took a shit on ours? They have all of space . . . they have everywhere to go." Slugger suddenly felt a strange sense of déjà vu that refused to leave him. Carli . . . he recalled saying something similar to her. She smiled in his thoughts, until her bloody remains flashed back and consumed his mind. The warlord froze and was trapped in memory until the car halted and his captor exited the vehicle.

They had reached an on-ramp that led onto a raised highway held up by cracked pillars and drenched in greenery. Parts of the highway were missing but strong vines twisted like cords over the road and filled in the open gaps. The road was littered with strange white cones grouped in threes. At a closer glance,

Slugger realized they consisted of a silky weblike thread, woven together to form the cone shapes. The Huntress approached the two tied up in the back. Without a word, she draped sacks over their heads.

"Fuck!" Slugger screamed. The Huntress immediately took his off to face him. She was slightly startled and annoyed at the outburst. She only looked at him, cold and curious, and said nothing. He eyed her callously. After a moment she scoffed and put the sack back over his head.

"This is for your own good," the Huntress then hissed. Reaching in her pocket, she pulled out a black face mask; thicker and snugger than a common surgical mask, and with a plastic, circular filter by the mouth. Once she put it on, she gave Ceteris a wink and got back in the truck. The Huntress looked ahead before strapping on a pair of goofy looking goggles.

The truck stubbornly hauled itself up the ramp, spitting black smog from behind and crackling like an old man. When a wheel rolled over one of the patches of green stitched over a break in the road, it sunk, almost as if it had rolled onto a thin grassy paper that was ready to give out at any moment. But it was surprisingly hardy, enduring the same treatment from the back tire as it did from the front.

The triplets of silky cones were too numerous to avoid, and the Huntress doublechecked her mask, making sure nothing could get in. As the vehicle bumped into its first trio of cones, they seemed to deflate and wither immediately. As they did, poisonous clouds of white dust spewed from the top openings like dry volcanos.

The Huntress squinted from underneath the protective goggles. As they trudged through and made contact with the cones littering the lonely highway, they spewed and spewed until her clothes and the vehicle were completely powdered in white. Their surroundings seemed to vanish, and for a moment, it seemed they had climbed to the sky and were level with the clouds.

Ceteris was unfazed, as his power suit filtered his breath. The alien was used to a slightly higher concentration of oxygen in his air, and despite the alterations of the landscape and its flora and fauna to make the land more familiar to his kind, the air remained roughly twenty percent oxygen. Because of this, it was hard for the Vagantem to breathe without the apparatus attached to his armor. No human had ever seen Ceteris without his battle suit, not even the Huntress. Inside the mechanized casing, he was immune to almost anything.

His armor and clear helmet were powdered with poisonous dust and his head seemed a faceless snowman's. Even the focus canon controlled by his tentacled mouth was caked with the stuff. Despite this, he was still able to see. The digital interface projected within the bubble led the way. It even highlighted shapes amidst the clouds that could easily be mistaken as dusty particles, but once magnified wriggled legs around like a spider would.

"Spore spiders, or lung spiders, some call 'em." The Huntress spoke loudly, intending the words for Slugger, but not really caring if he heard or not. "A parasitic colony of creatures that construct poisonous contraptions that not only slow and sicken those who breathe this miasma, but also lets them ride up into the air and implant themselves into the mucous membranes of larger beasts . . . meaning us, where they would feed, breed, and die. A whole generation inside of you . . . in less than a week."

Slugger listened carefully, though he was blinded by the sack over his head. “Hm,” he grunted with a forced and dull curiosity.

“Then you begin to decay from the inside.”

After an hour, the highway finally began to descend back into a network of intersecting streets and roadways that resembled a grid made up of broken asphalt and shrubbery. With the road's descent, the cones finally began to grow less numerous, and the noxious mist waned.

A nozzle lifted from Ceteris's wrist and he sprayed them down with pressurized air. The Huntress reached back and snatched the mask off her captive before removing her own protection.

In the near distance, right in front of a setting sun, sat a mighty metropolis. It was grand and glorious, though it seemed to be at the very precipice of either life or death. While the city continued to rot, signs of growth and life anew were prevalent. The highways entering from all sides made the city seem like a fat spider caught in its own web. A thin channel of shadow ran around the bastion of lights dazzling in the center, and a veil of smoke lay atop the streets and cozied the buildings; broken and battered, but still proud and standing. Laughter, music, screams, and shouts carried over on the wind. Slugger brooded with this. What was his canyon to this city?

Chapter VII – The Conspirator

They stopped just as the road leveled out. Ahead was a large double arch that stood over both sides of the freeway. In large red letters across its face, it read: "*Welcom_ to NEW B__ke-_hire City.*" There were a few letters missing, and the "*NEW*" was obviously recently painted in.

"We're here," said the Huntress with a faint smile as she exited the vehicle. Slugger remained quiet. He was impressed, blank, and placated. There was so much to see and hear and smell. He had no words and had begun to accept his fate—until he felt an irritated Ben shifting behind him.

"Can you take his hood off? I would like to convene with my associate," the captive warlord asked, his tone both snarky and dignified. The Huntress kept her smile, but before she walked over to remove the giant's blindbag, she shot a venomous glare toward Slugger. The smile lessened the glare's impact, but did nothing to ease the poison. There was something about her that made him nervous and uneasy.

When she lifted the sack off of Ben, he strangely seemed not to notice. Dusk light pushed through his bangs, but he did not even flinch. "What do you think, my friend?" asked Slugger. Ben was silent, though not in Slugger's head. ". . . What is that supposed to mean? You—" Before the warlord could finish, an alien aircraft emerged from the clouds and zoomed past the city, only to slowly descend toward a lonely mountain in the distance. Staring at the mountain, Slugger noticed faint lights blinking at its peak. He was so distracted that he did not notice the group of city officials waiting at the base of the arches.

The Huntress did not initially catch them either, but when she did, she rolled her eyes. She hopped back in the truck and drove up to meet them. There were two men and a woman, each with a clipboard, a pen, and a thick packet of documents. They were all in clean, pressed suits, looking almost alien to the two captives. Slugger was confused, and the loud crunching steps of Ceteris further flurried his thoughts. The Vagantem walked up to stand by the Huntress and to meet the receiving party.

"Huntress, Ceteris. We are glad to see you make it back in one piece," the man in the middle remarked while eyeing the two tied up in the truck.

"Who are they?" the woman to the left asked, wasting no time. Her sleeves were rolled up and Slugger noticed a tattoo on her arm, a black barcode next to an alien symbol.

"Strangers," the Huntress snapped back sharply.

"And what do you intend to do with these strangers?" the woman continued. This time she did not make eye contact with the Huntress and instead began to scribble down notes.

"I intend to sell them."

The three recipients looked at each other and then began to scratch down additional notes. "Sell them?" the man in the middle reiterated.

"Yes." The Huntress's smile was long gone, and her patience began running thin.

"I'm guessing they have not gone through identification yet?"

the middle man asked bluntly.

"What do you think?" said the Huntress.

"Always so testy," said the woman as she scrawled more into her packet. The Huntress gave her a look that forced the woman to nervously clear her throat.

"Testy," repeated Ceteris.

"If you'd like, we can take you to the identification center," said the man in the middle, and he seemed genuine in his offer.

"Oh, fuck off. You don't think that's the first place I'm going to? Come on, Ceteris," the Huntress said as she walked back to the truck.

"You cannot enter without our return evaluation!" the woman barked at the Huntress, who seemed to care little about this group of individuals and their processes. The man who stood quietly on the right rested his hand on the woman's shoulder and shook his head. Afterward, she held back any objections.

Ceteris strode on, leading the way as the battered truck retched and spit its way forward. Slugger met the eyes of the silent man on the right as they drove by. The woman and the man on the left were busy jotting down notes. A strip of shade washed over the truck as they passed under the arches. Then he noticed, hidden behind brush and rubble, a pack of gunmen at the ready, no longer concealing themselves. Slugger looked around, paranoid; every sound and sense of movement itched his skull. They had now entered the city of New Blake-Shire.

The outskirts seemed hollow and empty at first, dark and desolate, with more ruin than identifiable structure. Suddenly a short, round woman passed by quietly using a longbow as a walking stick. A quiver of arrows hung over her shoulder. There seemed to be no one else around until the crowds sounded up ahead, and they could feel the lights. Skyscrapers poked purple clouds gleaming with moonlight, sprawling apartment buildings never ended, and great billboards of the past had been repurposed into advertisements for fights, local bands, and gladiators. Few streetlights remained flickering, but large blazing pits placed along street corners tried to stay the night. Blast zone craters, fire stains, and deep cracks along the city roads and structures could not be erased, but they could be—and were—ignored.

Once they reached the inner workings of the city, it was hard to avoid pedestrians and other vehicles. Salesmen and entertainers desperately sought the attention of any passersby. The Huntress ignored them, and had to swing her door open several times to smack pesky salesmen off from clinging to the sides.

There was a madness in these people, a hunger and thirst for more than just sustenance. "Batteries! I've got all types, and they're fresh," pleaded a scraggly trader before he was knocked down. The Huntress ran the man's leg over, but his pained wails were ignored amongst the bustling city life. Another Vagantem, suited with armor and artillery faintly similar to that of Ceteris, was on patrol. A drone no larger than a football buzzed around his head like an incessant fly before fitting back into the armor's back plating.

It was too much. Slugger wanted to observe and study just about everything in this place. The constant movement prevented this; the noise blinded him, and the smell and smoke lacked nostalgia. He'd grown accustomed to the strange lands of his limited empire; not this relic of society. Not this city brought back from the dead. It seemed to him a cheap shortcut to his long-term vision. "They're gonna eat you!" blasted a dirty old woman who then began to maniacally point and cackle at the tied-up pair.

Eventually, they arrived at a small government building guarded with spiked rails and barbed wire. It was sandwiched between two apartment complexes raised with brick and wrapped in fire escape ladders. A group of armed men stalked the block, studying all who got too close. Their eyes stayed focused on the incoming truck—until they recognized the driver.

"I got some boys who need IDs!" the Huntress shouted. One man in a ski mask rolled his hand inward, directing her to park by the gate. He kept his finger on the trigger of a sawed-off shotgun; it had notches in the handle.

"Huntress." The name strained through Ceteris's voice modulator as he approached. Still, she could tell his tone was grave and sober. The Vagantem moved to the driver's side of the truck, and she looked at him, waiting. "I must go," he finally said. Even the alien could tell she was disappointed. The Huntress only nodded, and off the warrior went.

Ceteris's pace picked up. He pushed through crowds with no regard for any humans obstructing his path. At times, he would swing his long metal arms to swipe several people away. Most knew to stay clear, though there were always casualties. After a long trudge, Ceteris finally reached a black building. Steel bars sealed the windows and a Vagantem drone monitored the vicinity, flying circles and drawing a false halo in the sky with its trail of light.

Two Vagantem guards were stationed at the front entrance. The red metal of their armor and weaponry glinted with light from the bright city. The metal, bloodsilver, looked newer and cleaner than the golden sunmetal suit that clad Ceteris. As he approached, the guards immediately moved aside to allow him entry. Ceteris ignored them.

As he stepped inside, he was met by another Vagantem, one who chose not to wear a warrior's battle suit. This Vagantem was a bureaucrat and dressed instead in a stardust coat. Resembling a dumbbell, the sophisticated breathing apparatus was tucked between his tentacles and just over his mouth, but left the majority of his blue skin exposed. Without the power armor, the alien's true size was revealed. Despite the hulking mass of their suits, the Vagantem were a small species, averaging around three-and-a-half to five feet tall. And they were a frail people, due to an evolutionary dependence on technology. Behind their oval craniums, small horns, almost unnoticeable, stuck out at the bottom of the skull, cradling the soft, heavy heads as they slumped downward. The horns were relatively new adaptions, having formed only a few hundred generations ago to help keep their bulky heads balanced and to relieve stress off their scrawny necks.

The two met eyes before Ceteris bowed. His head remained lowered until the bureaucrat touched the top of his helmet, allowing him to stand again. *"Warden,"* Ceteris said respectfully in his true tongue. When Ceteris spoke his own language, he seemed different. His voice and words were less naïve and more heavy with disdain.

"Ceteris," the warden replied, cool and calculated.

"You know why I'm here."

"Yes, I do. However, I am not sure you know why he is here," said the warden.

"Will you prevent me?" asked Ceteris, his tone eager.

"No." The warden stood proud, and a few Vagantem bureaucrats and guards in the sally port watched the interaction

anxiously.

"Good." The armored giant stormed past him and stomped to a dark hallway. The warden eyed Ceteris curiously before dropping his gaze and returning to his quarters. Ceteris continued, going deeper within the prison. Guards allowed him through, wanting no trouble from this particular Vagantem. It took quite some time to reach the end: a pitch-black hole that caged but one inmate. Another guard stood by the last gate before the cell, and immediately unlocked it for the arriving guest.

"Leave us," demanded Ceteris. Before the guard left, he bowed low, similar to how Ceteris had bowed for the Warden. Ceteris eyed him, then rested his suit's hand gently atop the other Vagantem's helmet.

Silence remained until Ceteris and the prisoner were alone. There was no light; the area was empty blackness. Then came the sound of iron rings knocking on the bars. *"Ceteris, Prime General."* These words did not flow through a modulator or breathing apparatus. They were raw and strained, but enduring.

"What have I told you about calling me that?" said Ceteris.

"You will always be a general," stated the prisoner. He then began to inhale strenuously through a tube hooked to a stationary machine.

Ceteris paused for a moment. Then he kneeled and bowed. *"You will always be our star teller."*

There was a drag of chains deep within the shadows. *"I cannot reach you."* Ceteris stood angrily after hearing this. *"It's alright, General. I won't be here for long."*

"Yes, you will be," Ceteris refuted. Silence followed. *"He was not on that ship . . . he lives still, commanding our Vagan,"* he

continued.

"I know. We must go with plan three. Where have you been? What is your counsel?" the prisoner was polite but deadly serious. Before Ceteris could answer, he noticed the monitoring system hovering just below the ceiling. It was silent and nearly invisible in the dark, but Ceteris's interface highlighted it for him. *"That has been taken care of. We are truly alone, and in the dark,"* confirmed the prisoner.

". . . The fleet is in lockdown. Security measures are tightening. It will be harder to move."

"As to be expected. This event has at least soured his image. We can gain sympathy from this."

"Over one hundred thousand were aboard Mercy. *Women, younglings . . . No more talk of sacrifice, not when Vagantem are dying. I will take no part in that path. The humans, though—"* Ceteris began, but was cut off.

"No, not yet. You have old friends, generals and patriots, who have begun to have second thoughts about their current leader. I have heard whispers from the chambers. Morale is fading; the stars in their eyes are dwindling. His reign will not last. Some of the guards are with us too; even this warden has thought on my offers."

"Who are these generals?" asked Ceteris.

"Your best friend, and our father's enemy." Silence overcame Ceteris as he considered this.

"I have found a way to get you out," said Ceteris. *"I have found a doctor, and an engineer."*

"Who?"

"Pax Leosine and Rada Phasm."

"And you trust them."

"Yes."

"Was this trust easily found? Did your worry for me cloud any

judgement?" said the prisoner, almost humorously.

"No . . . Pax and Rada are ready. And my old legion remains loyal." Ceteris remained serious.

"Be patient, General."

"I cannot! He has made that pool swimmer general of my legion. He scatters them, purposefully wasting their time, keeping them away from the fleet. I hear whispers too, that my Vagan are disappearing, especially those who speak out. We will soon lose our only force," Ceteris's disdain turned fearful and sad.

". . . These are good Vagan, patriots and star soldiers," said the prisoner solemnly.

"Did you know?" asked Ceteris, his tone slipping into anger.

"I heard a rumor. Maybe you're right; no more sacrifices. The deaths of our Vagan need to stop. What about the humans did you want to share?" asked the prisoner.

"There is a group out there, wild men with weapons. I was working with the Huntress and we took in two of theirs."

"Why would I spare a second thought for a group of wild humans?" asked the prisoner, almost breaking his formality.

"No one knows about this group except for me. Not even the Huntress."

"How?"

"The two we have are liars, concealing their friends . . . I think they are spies. I went back and tracked them and found many signs of a wild group; bullet holes, footprints, even graves. Then I sent my wing. The drone followed a small group and it found others, many others. They seemed to be mobilizing an attack; they might know of this city. They built an impressive fortress, in spite of the wild in them. My wing remains there, watching from the clouds. I can see them now, moving and working." Ceteris shifted his attention to the footage uploading to his interface.

"I see. And you sense a possible ally? What about this Huntress?" The prisoner's tone turned taunting. *"You seem to be keeping this from her for some reason."*

"She will be of use, soon," said Ceteris.

"Keep an eye on them, but remember to think of the larger picture. If I must stay in here for a little longer then so be it. Focus on your own Vagan. Keep your eyes on the stars."

Chapter VIII – City of the Damned

"This mother fucker will be a gladiator god," said the man in the ski mask as the Huntress pulled up.

"Oh yeah, he'll rape in the ring, then he'll go straight to the Bowl," said the Huntress.

"Who's the other guy?" the man asked.

"Just some dude," the Huntress scoffed.

"Hm. Here . . . blood-testers are on their way." The man handed her a form and a pencil. She exited the car and used the hard surface of the hood to hold the form. She then began reading the questions.

"#1: Name"

"Hey buddy . . . what's your and the big guy's names?" she asked her captive.

"Slugger and Big Ben," stated the defeated warlord. She then began to scrawl a messy scratch of barely legible letters.

"#1: Name – Slugger, Ben"

"#2: Where – Huego's Farm"

"#3: Encounter – They approached the farmhouse with dead poacher, Alex Bolt. Admitted to killing the rest of the poachers out of self-defense. Claimed they tried to save Alex and did not want to kill the others. Alex disclosed location of New Blake-Shire."

"#4: ID Type – Fighter and Poacher"

"#5: Accountability – I, _________, take full responsibility of my guest until his or her ID is issued. I will remain as second contact and prioritize helping city officials and Vagantem authorities with any request regarding this individual. Failure to adhere to this will result in punishment up to and including imprisonment, termination, and exile."

The Huntress read the last item curiously. The forms seemed to get more and more vague every time she had to fill one out. She signed it, almost reluctantly, as Maisie O'Brien.

An alien drone hovered its way over to the small crowd huddled around the truck. It did not look like the speedy, copter-like monitor drones called wings, but rather a floating orb. At the center was a white eye of light that peeked through metal plates and clear plastic. The light flickered and made the drone seem to blink. Those who knew of its origin and purpose moved out of the way. It flew up to the Huntress and scanned her, then flew over to the bed of the truck and eyed the tied-up pair. The eye suddenly opened up like a mouth, slowly. Out came a thin metal arm, and at the tip, a needle so ghostly sharp and thin it seemed to appear and disappear at various angles. Its translucent edging mirrored off of Slugger's wide eyes, and the image screamed at him like a banshee in his mind. Ben remained unmoving, and the warlord flinched for him.

The orb stuck the silent giant first, in the side of the neck. There was a squirt of blood as the needle slid back out, but then the prick point seemed to bubble, and the flow of blood ceased. Slugger watched in horror, but before he could express this, another blood-tester drone outside his periphery pricked him in a similar area. The two were immediately rendered unconscious. The blood-testers pulled back their metal arms and shut their mouth-like openings once the needles were concealed. The white eyes resumed glowing, and the orbs began to buzz and beep as if uploading data. Soon after, they flew away, toward the mountain.

The Huntress understood their fear and remembered how similarly scared she was, once. Despite the tedious bureaucracy, bringing in newcomers brought a form of satisfaction for her. She knew they'd be fine, mostly. The thought of a man being so desperate and scared had made her sad at one point in her life. Now, it made her smile. It was comical, but beyond that, it was fascinating. How their eyes would darken and shrink, how their breath would speed and slow, how their skin grew moist and pale; she enjoyed all of it. She'd even begun to notice a recurring smell and taste in the air that all the fearful emitted. Never did she feel any guilt for this.

"Can I pick 'em up tomorrow morning?" asked the Huntress as a group of men struggled to carry an out-cold Slugger and Ben.

"Most likely the day after, but not here," said the ski-masked leader. He scribbled an address down on a piece of scratch paper with a black sharpie: "*1137 Telecom Ln, Unit #3*," and gave it to her. "This is the new pickup facility," said the man gruffly. The Huntress nodded. "They have any gear or supplies?" he then asked.

"Oh, right. Over here." In the passenger seat lay two duffle bags; Ben's mace handle stuck out of one. Two men reached for the bags through the missing door, but before they took them, the Huntress clicked her tongue to get their attention. "I know exactly what's in there." As she left, her trail of smog lingered in the city night.

She found a five-story parking garage with plenty of spaces

open. The walls were aged and cracked, but the rails were painted with a fresh brick red. As she entered, she could see the manager chasing a young adolescent down the entrance ramp. The man was swinging a baseball bat, and the youth seemed to thrive on the adrenaline. "Get out of here, you fucking scrapper! I'll fucking kill you!" the man shouted. The teenager was able to escape out the driveway, even with the Huntress blocking most of it with the farmer's truck. Her brow was raised.

The manager was panting and sweating. As he wiped the sweat from his forehead, he greeted her. "Welcome miss, looking for space to leave this thing?"

"Mmhm," she confirmed.

"Well, look no further. The Vagantem patrol will be back this way soon and the scrappers will be scared off. 'Til then, I'll make sure no one lays a finger on this beaut." His smile was obviously stressed and unsure.

"Wouldn't call it a beaut myself," said the Huntress. The man smiled wider at this, and his stress seemed to lighten.

"It needs some work for sure, but this thing has potential," said the man.

"Want it?" asked the Huntress. She was distracted, and in a rush. The man's jaw dropped.

"I barely have the pebbles to afford something even in this shape," he admitted.

"How much would you give me if you did?"

"Umm . . . I don't know. Maybe . . . a hundred?"

"Sold."

"Miss . . . I don't have that." The man was confused, and his stress returned in full force.

"You should at some point . . . right?" she asked, cool and

coy. The man did not answer. He began to have a sneaking suspicion that he was being played with.

"I do not have time for this," he snapped.

She tossed the keys to him. "I have no use for it now. Take it. Keep your pebbles. I will only ask one thing of you: remember my face, and my name." The man stared at her in amazement. Before she was gone, he realized he'd forgotten to ask for her name.

"Excuse me, miss!" he shouted over to her. "What is your name?"

"Huntress."

* * *

Not far from the garage, there was a collective blare of noise and movement. Crowds rushed violently toward the stadium. The Blake-Shire Bowl, it was called; the largest football stadium in the world. The lights were so bright that all the surrounding stars were blotted out, and even the black sky was lifted to a lighter shade. The moon remained, purple and plump, but now had competition from the grounded world. Horns blew, cheers roared, and the raucous audience abused the chain-link fencing encasing the field, sending waves of rattles and clanks.

The Huntress did not enter through the front entrance, where the swaths of spectators funneled in. Instead, she went to a small gate off to the side, where two vibrant trees stood guard. To the left was a red maple with a green birdhouse hanging off a high branch. To the right was a blue spruce, sharp and frosted. They were the last of their natural lines; any others in their likeness seen around the world were nothing more than artificial.

The small gate was less impressive than the main entrance, and easily scalable. The Huntress pulled out a key from her sneaker, opened the door, then locked up again once she was in. Down a short tunnel, she met a strange door that looked as if it had been installed recently. It was a dark mahogany, rough and splintered to the touch. At its center was a brass Native American face. The feathered headwear sprouted upward, and the detailed lines, chiseled masterfully, made the man's face stern and kingly. Attached below the face was a U-shaped brass knocker that dug its pointed ball into the door. The Huntress lifted it and slammed it once, then twice.

A moment later, she was greeted by a thin woman. The woman had piercings strewn all over her face, and she wobbled on a peg leg. "This ain't your night," said the woman hoarsely.

"I'm just here to watch . . . and maybe sign up for another bout," said the Huntress. The thin woman's twisted smile was disheartening.

"You are one nasty bitch, you know that?" asked the woman playfully. The Huntress only smiled. "Go and enjoy yourself. I'll find a good match for you," said the woman, softer this time as she opened another door and directed her in. The Huntress gave her a coy wink as she passed by.

The tunnel led up to the stadium's VIP box seating. She entered with a confidence that caught the attention of some of the others. She sat at the last row, on the far left. The window had cracks and there were bullet holes along the walls. Still, this was infinitely better than the common seats and nosebleeds outside, and there was a bar behind the two rows of seats. In the VIP box seating were other successful fighters and hunters, along with inventors, doctors, politicians, and some of the city's finest entertainers. There were no Vagantem around, however.

This was human entertainment.

Outside the window, the great football stadium was topped with a dome of chain-link fencing, preventing the audience from disturbing the events. The field itself looked alien; it was a small desert, artificial and contained. The strange rock formations and prickly plant life dazzled under the high intensity lighting.

Suddenly, a band started to play music. They were a cover band and played the songs of the dead world; ancient art that was not easily forgotten. The stage was opposite from the entrance, and set up around the edge of the stage were long, cannon-like tubes that spit out lashes of flame and shot up colorful bombs of fire, decorating the night and shrouding the beyond. Over the speakers, an irritating voice announced. "No need for an introduction on this one, I assume. Here's Father!"

Thunderous applause and praise momentarily overcame the music and shook the world. The Huntress stared curiously at the man entering the arena. His bald head was darkened by the specks of returning hair. Dark brown eyes, almost black, looked straight, as if he could only see and hear what was ahead of him. He had a patchy goatee and a face full of tattoos that listed his past association with and devotion to an old-world criminal family. Most notably of all, and what gave him his name, Father, was his attire: black slacks with not a crinkle or crease, a black clerical shirt with a spot of white where the tab collar was seen, and a large iron cross dangling off a silver chain around his neck. In one hand he carried a Bible, holding it closely to his chest, and in the other was an old sword, its tip scraping along the sand.

Down in the arena in the fake desert, Father spoke to himself, "Lord, give me strength. My fate is at your will." On the other side of the arena was a drawbridge gate. Behind it came a whistle and scream of such pure horror that the band stopped playing and the crowd fell silent and breathless. It was not human—the woolly banshee is what they called it. When Father saw the name on the bout list, it had sent a chill down his spine. The scream, however, stopped his heart and made him feel him ill. "Lord, look after me."

The gate lifted and a slow thud of footsteps could be heard before the creature blundered out. It was bipedal and slightly humanoid. Its limbs were thin and bony, but its feet and hands were strong and heavy. Upon its head was a crown of antlers, sharp and evil, and sprouting out from its elbows were two long horns. Upon its chest, belly, and back were thick patches of grey woollen locks. The creature was silent as it pierced Father with its white, soulless eyes. Its mouth was elongated, like an anteater's, and its long red tongue whipped and whirled around as if it was tasting the air. Suddenly, the mouth opened up and strings of bloody drool stretched across its gaping maw. The scream came again, like a gale of death, and choked up all who witnessed it.

Father held his ground, shaking and sweating. The creature charged, slashing its claws through the air and screaming bloody terror. He put the Bible gently down in the sand and gripped his sword with both hands. The metal tip glinted with the stage's light. "I fear . . . no evil. I fear none but God himself," the priest said while gritting his teeth. The beast was already halfway through the stadium when he realized its true height. It would take three of him to meet its gaze. He was not prepared, but he would not back down. The man turned and ran, leaving the Bible behind.

As the priest began heading for the chain-link barriers, the crowd began to boo and curse him with only the occasional supportive comment.

"Coward!"

"You got this, Father!"

"I bet all the pebbles in the world on you, asshole!"

He had no trouble ignoring this; all his attention was on the beast still charging him. It was getting closer, running on two legs like a human. He held his sword with his teeth, biting into the steel. The blade cut the edges of his lips, sending a red trickle down his neck. He reached the fencing and started to climb. The boos were still there but many shushed and watched curiously. The priest managed to reach thirty feet before the fence was pounded on from below. The banshee had made it.

First, it violently shook the fencing, ringing its long claws into the chain links futilely, but its prey wasn't coming down. Then it stretched its arms out desperately, but the man kept climbing. The creature finally decided to try to climb as well. Despite its nimble appearance, the beast's massive size and awkward shape made the attempt a struggle.

It became distracted for a split second, and then a deadly flash was upon it. The father had let go of the chain dome as he reached the curve. As he fell, he stabbed his blade downward through the banshee's hollow crown of thorns, piercing through the brain and down its throat. He collapsed with the monster in a horrible impact. The antlers skewered his arm, and he lay there bloody with the beast as first responders rushed to the scene. The crowd went wild, with some even brought to tears in relief. The suspense was what they came for. The Huntress smiled devilishly as she clapped along with the others in the VIP box.

* * *

Later that night, the Huntress entered her lonely little house, dilapidated but still livable, on the outskirts of the city. She was greeted by a feline meowing nonstop. “Okay, okay, come on Peas. Time to eat.”

Chapter IX – A Night Out

Slugger awoke in a padded cell. The room, once white, was a stained yellow. He was alone, no longer tied to his enforcer, though he was still tied up. He was parched and found that he had urinated all over himself in his daze. His clothes were filthy and ripped, and now cold and wet. As he sat there thinking of all the cruel things he would do to these people when given a chance, he noticed that the skin on his forearm stung. He tried to forget it; he could not take a look, as it was tied up behind him. "Benny, Ben, Ben . . . Ben Ben, Big Ben, Big Benny Ben." The warlord, in a deranged and hungry state, began to sing and hallucinate.

"Here," said a man through a slit in the door as he slid in a plate of food. The plate carried a bundle of green beans, a wet spongy cake, and a nameless crisped critter. Slugger laughed aloud. "Give me your hands," said the man with a stone voice.

It took Slugger a moment to realize what was happening, but the man was patient. The warlord eventually stood and walked over to the door. He turned around and bent over, sticking his restrained wrists through the slit. The man sliced through them with a knife and left without a word. Slugger stared at the food before devouring it. He had to cough up a bone at one point, and it was then he noticed his new tattoo: an alien glyph like a crescent moon with codes and lettering huddled around it. The sight made him sick with rage. His left eye began to twitch, but his face remained blank. In thought, he sat there. Still, he did not have a barcode like the woman at the arches. Though this was little comfort, it stoked his interest.

"Looks like you need some cleaning up. How about a night on the town . . . hm?" The Huntress stared at him through the slit.

He hadn't heard her coming, which bothered him more than he cared to admit, but he obscured his momentary shock with a nasty smile.

* * *

As a crew of hazmat suits sprayed the warlord's naked body clean with a powerful hose in a room not too far off, the Huntress filled out more paperwork. "This one's got Hep A, and the big ass one's got a brain tumor the size of my fist," said the examiner as he flipped through his notebook.

"I just need the talker for now," said the Huntress.

"Yes, yes. He's almost ready. Now, when are you going to pick up the big guy?" asked the examiner anxiously. His glasses were fogged, and his coat was not kept clean. His bald head poked out above a ring of fading hair like a snowy peak. His eyes would squint, then open up wide before squinting again. The examiner did this repeatedly, without fail, as he spoke.

"Give me another day or two, eh?" asked the Huntress with both a wicked and warm smile.

"Yes, yes," said the man as his eyes darted back to his documents; squinting and opening, squinting and opening.

Slugger dried off with a towel and dressed in the outfit he

came in with. His shirt remained blood-streaked, but it smelled cleaner, and it was dry. His pants were clean too. However, his belt, which had held his silent sisters, and his knife-toed boots were still unreturned. Instead he was given a pair of sneakers, slightly too small for him. Then, something happened he did not expect; something so strange that he did not know how to react. After watching him dress, the hazmat guards opened the door and directed him out, freely and unrestrained. Each step was reluctant and suspicious, however, the guards did not attempt anything, and they closed the door behind him and began to sterilize the cleaning room.

He walked down a lit and lonely hallway until he was forced to turn. At the turn, he found the Huntress talking with the examiner.

"There he is," said the examiner.

"You ready?" she asked Slugger.

"Yes, yes," the examiner answered for him.

"Where is Ben?" asked the warlord with a brazen fire inside.

"He'll be leaving soon, it's just you and me tonight." The Huntress's smile seemed inviting, and yet also cruel.

* * *

The nightlife was smokey and excited. People were everywhere, in every nook and cranny of the city. Vehicles struggled to navigate the sea of moving faces. Lights blinded and created perfect pockets of shadow. Crossing the street amongst the crowd was tedious, but once the two made it, Slugger and the Huntress looked up to see a blazing billboard of light atop a busy nightclub. A constant stream of people were entering and exiting. A man laughed hysterically as his friend drunkenly vomited by a large dumpster. He then pushed his friend into the pile of bile and ran away cackling. The man struggled to get up, soaked and splashing in his own regurgitation.

After an hour of little conversation, the two reached the entrance. They met a bodyguard at the front. He was clad in black leather, and his slicked-back hair blended in with his attire. A fat golden chain hung just below his double chin. The man was almost a perfect circle, but still tall and strong. He had an alien scanning device that had a handle similar to a gun's. Aiming it at Slugger's new tattoo, it read it like a code. It beeped and flashed a small blue and green light.

"Come on in, you're good," said the man in an accent that originated from across the ocean, on an island in the Pacific.

As the two entered, it seemed they had changed worlds. The lighting was no longer white, but blue. The shade was almost sensual, and the depraved minds of those inside sped up. The music was so deafening that the bass smacked them with its beat and the synths felt as if they could shatter glass. Still, the song was sweet and happy. Slugger saw a short man with a spiky head humping one of the high speakers. The man seemed just about ready to finish when a guard grabbed him by the collar and dragged him out.

The Huntress grabbed the warlord's arm, who flinched, and pulled him toward the center of the dance floor. Suddenly, a pale flash of flesh ran by. Two young women, beautiful and intoxicated, ran through the dance floor, holding hands and completely naked. They giggled and soon began to skip. As Slugger watched them, two men bumped into him from behind.

One was a fat pasty man whose folds and flabs luckily hung over his manhood. He was naked and pinching his hands in the air as if they were crab claws. The other was clad in nothing but a pair of boots and a stained pair of white briefs. In his hands, he proudly waved the American flag. "For freedom!" he blasted as the two playfully chased the young women. Slugger chuckled at the comedic scene.

The Huntress began to dance to the electronic beat, confident and elegant. She attempted to grab his hands, but he pulled them back, almost violently. The warlord was at a loss. He began feeling increasingly uncomfortable. "No," he plainly stated.

The Huntress only smiled. "Fine, let's not waste time. Come on," she said as she waved him over to one of the side tables. After they sat, the Huntress just stared at him with a twisted lip, waiting for him to speak first.

"What?" he asked.

"Ben, is it?" Slugger nodded at this. "I need him to win three fights." Slugger cocked his brow, unamused. "He is a monster, and easy pebbles."

"What in the fuck are pebbles?" he asked hotly.

"Money . . . it's the Vagantem's currency; the gift of an economy." As she spoke, she pulled out a black-blue marble. Inside, like a fossil trapped in sap, was a small metal face in the likeness of a great Vagantem leader. The tendrils of its face held on to stars, each a different size. Slugger stared at it as he tried to contain his amazement. The Huntress studied his face as he looked.

"Three fights, huh?" asked Slugger. "When do we become free citizens?"

"*You* are," she said sharply. "You are free to enter and leave as you please. You can trade, participate in recreation, and settle down in one of the unclaimed living spaces."

"And yet, I don't feel free."

The Huntress belched a laugh. "Who cares how you feel? Go on and see for yourself."

"Hm. What about Ben?" he asked.

"I asked them to keep him just a bit longer so we could have this talk." Her eyes were piercing. The warlord stared at her, trying not to grind his teeth. "And if the talk doesn't go the way I want it to, then he may never get out."

"Just tell me what you want," said Slugger tiredly.

"Three fights. Convince him to win all and I'll make sure you two are living like me. Like kings." Something in the warlord glinted, and as she noticed the change, her smile fell flat. The warlord smiled, and his psycho eyes opened so widely that the air wrung tears from them. The whole display took her off guard.

"Like the kings of hell?"

She only stared at him, furrowing her brows. "Sure."

After a few songs, they remained at the table, with no further words to share. "I'll be right back." Another song began, and this time it was slower and less hectic. When the Huntress returned, she was not alone. She was with a woman, barely in her mid-twenties. Her hair, if she had any, was hidden underneath a bright pink wig that stopped at her shoulders. Her face was dolled up with plenty of makeup and her outfit seemed purposefully revealing.

"This is Dixie. Be nice, both of you. I have a big night tomorrow and gotta get some rest," said the Huntress in a tired voice.

"You gonna be fightin' tomorrow?" asked Dixie in a sweet voice.

"Mmhm." The Huntress nodded.

"Jesus. You're insane," said Dixie in admiration.

Slugger stared at the pair, angry and anxious, but patient—he must be patient. He smiled at Dixie, and she smiled back coyly. "Come on. Let's go to the basement floor," she said.

The Huntress studied her, then looked back to Slugger. "You gonna be okay without me?" she asked.

"I will be now," he said politely as he shot another glance to the sparkle-eyed girl. She almost giggled. Her cheeks were rosy, and this cutesy act was a clear attempt to make her appear more innocent than she probably was. The warlord took this into consideration, but he played along. The Huntress tapped the warlord and handed him several pebbles with a wink. She was then off without a word, swift as the evening wind.

When she exited, she saw Ceteris by the entrance. "What are you doing here?" she asked sharply with a cold smile.

"Here . . . I am just keeping an eye out," he said plainly.

"I got a fight tomorrow. You gonna come see it?" Ceteris saw the excitement of a child in her eyes. Stars began to swell in his.

"Of course," he said, and she smiled at this, slightly warmer this time. She was gone in an instant, and Ceteris watched her leave, looking as if he had much more to say.

* * *

"Come on then," Dixie ordered innocently as she pulled on his hand. He followed her, his face hurting from fake smiling. She led him through a curtain and down a stair path in the corner. The stairway was dark, and it seemed to be absorbing many different forms of sound waves and drums before echoing back an unintelligible cacophony.

At the bottom level, they were met with a yellow door, and

Dixie wasted no time in opening it. On the other side, the songs were just as rowdy and stubborn, however, they were not electronic, and they were not in English. A Japanese band played a blend of pop and rock. The singer wore a large pair of shades and his ear flickered with a dangling disco ball earring. The bassist wore a gorilla mask and hairy gloves to match. The guitarist howled through a wolf mask, and his hungry movements seemed to resemble the animal's characteristics. The drummer was blindfolded, yet never missed a beat.

Slugger was impressed; he knew it would be a lie to deny this. He saw a bar off to the side and motioned with his head for the girl to follow. As soon as they sat, the bartender dropped two large mugs of bubbling brew in front of them, splashing them with foam. "No one drinks nothin' 'til they tell me what they think of my latest creation!" he shouted.

Dixie laughed as she wiped the splashed beer from her face. Slugger was less amused but followed her lead. "Cheers!" she roared before clinking mugs with the warlord. He forced yet another fake smile and felt as if they were losing their power. Still, the girl was acting sweet and naïve. They chugged their drinks. Dixie finished hers first. "Yum!"

"It's pretty good I guess," said Slugger, though he'd left most of the beverage intact, not wanting any buzz or impairment. The bartender smiled at both of them, then picked up a miniature keg full of his home brew and plopped it on the table for them to finish, freely. As he walked off to deal with other patrons, Dixie quickly reached over the bar and grabbed a thin bottle of whiskey.

"Come on," she said, sly and cautious. Through the dancing crowds, they found a ledge near the stage to sit. The Japanese band stopped playing and waved graciously to their fans before walking offstage. Another band entered, this time a group of grungy men who all clearly cared little about their appearance. The singer was misshapen; his arms were dwarflike and twisted. A headset atop his bleached hair brought a microphone close to his mouth. It was a pathetic sight to the warlord.

The music began, and a train of nostalgia smacked him into a daze. The guitar, just the guitar at first. Then the hi-hats trickled in. The drums with the bass, then the scratch of a DJ's disc . . . all of it, he knew. He knew this song.

As the rapper started, Slugger's ears twitched. This poetry was silken flame; smooth and hot to the touch. The song continued, and Slugger almost forgot who he was with. Suddenly, the noise ceased, all except the occasional slide up a bass string. And then the rapper pointed to the misshapen singer ecstatically in an attempt to hype up the crowd for the incoming solo.

The singer's voice was a raspy whisper. He repeated the same line with increasing intensity. After the fourth time, he amped his tune up and screamed with all his pain and might.

The singer dropped and began to flounder on the floor like a suffocating fish as he sang. The music, along with the singer, picked up. Elbows began flying and spurts of blood followed. Men were pushing, shoving, and throwing each other across the room. Dixie was getting nervous; the chaos was on its way to them. Slugger, however, remained in complete lionization, fawning over his rediscovered memories. She tried to snap him out of it, but it was no use. He remained, hypnotized. Dixie then caught sight of his teary eyes as he muttered, "A place . . . for my, head?" as if unsure of the song title that came to mind. She laughed.

"I remember them too. One of my favorite bands. These

aren't them obviously, but they sound pretty damn close. Come on, we are going to get trampled if we stay here." Dixie seemed to understand, as if it was difficult for her too, to hear the songs of the past. Slugger wiped his tears away and followed.

The two got knocked and bumped but never lost their feet. They were pushed up against a wall by the crowd. Dixie leaned in close to the warlord, then reached for his crotch. "How many pebbles can I earn tonight?" she asked with an emptiness in her eyes and a velvet tongue that curled its way around Slugger's ear. The warlord instinctually grabbed her wrist, then let go after realizing what was happening. She flinched but continued. Her hand began to snake its way down his pants, and then she grabbed his erect manhood. "I want to earn these pebbles baby, what do I gotta do?" she asked again, almost moaning with pleasure as the words left her lips.

She began to stroke him. "And why should I pay?" asked the warlord. She stopped and pulled her hand out of his jeans.

"I'm not free. Huntress only paid for the company, not the extra," she said sternly.

"Well, I'm not paying. I don't pay for sex. Who in the fuck do you think I am?" Slugger's malice accidentally slipped out in his tone.

"Ha! Okay then, keep on crying, you broke-ass fucking baby!" Dixie spat, and as she turned, Slugger yanked her by the back of the shirt.

"What was that?" he asked with an evil smirk. The girl almost fell as he pulled.

"Don't fucking touch me! Asshole!" she barked as she flailed her arms. The small girl tried to pull again, and this time Slugger let go immediately and she fell. "Oh, you're dead!" She scuffled off, pouting and embarrassed. Slugger watched her leave, then turned back to listen to yet another band. The mosh pit was subsiding as the music calmed.

Fifteen minutes later, Dixie returned with three large men. They surrounded the warlord, cornering him into the very same wall where the first altercation had occurred. Slugger saw them approaching and froze, staring at them with a ghostly numbness. "That's him," spat the angered girl.

"What kind of man touches a young lady, huh?" the largest of the brutes started off while the other two inched closer. Slugger scoffed and chuckled.

"Something funny, boy?" another asked.

"Kinda," taunted Slugger.

"And what is that?" asked the initial brute. No plan seeped into his thoughts; the warlord did not have his men to back him up, he did not have Ben to scare the big ones away, and he did not currently enjoy the company of his beloved beasts. He was truly alone.

"Look guys, I didn't hurt her. She's a big girl, she'll be fine," Slugger said.

The men all looked at each other, then at Dixie, and the group laughed. "I don't care if she's hurt or not . . . no one touches her." The leader had a permanent scowl, and lines of age and stress seamed his square face.

"Hmm . . . well, not without charge," snapped Slugger. The group grew angry at this, especially Dixie.

"Just kill him already," said the girl fervently. The men chortled and stepped closer in silent obedience. One grabbed Slugger by the neck and lifted him up against the wall. The warlord desperately clasped the man's wrists and tried to pull them away as he struggled, gasping for air. The one on the left took out a switchblade knife and drew a red, wet line down the warlord's cheek.

Suddenly, Slugger pulled the pressure off his neck and shoved a palm upward to the knife-wielder's face. He managed to turn the blade and thrust it back into the man's mouth, slicing through gum, lip, and teeth. The man collapsed in a bloody mess, holding his leaking face. Screams sounded off from all around, and a stampede of guests flushed out of the basement. Slugger wasn't finished.

In the immediate commotion, the warlord dropped to the floor and shot a fist at the leader's undefended groin. As the man fell to his knees, the third man locked the warlord into a chokehold.

"Not bad, not bad . . . you little fucker. You're gonna pay for that, I promise you," hissed the man as he squeezed harder and harder around Slugger's neck. Soon after, Slugger fell limp, and the man threw his unconscious body to the hard floor and began kicking him. It was sticky and bloody down there, but Slugger's senses were in and out.

Before Dixie and the enforcers knew what was happening, the surrounding crowd was cleared, and the basement was nearly empty. The music had stopped. Clicks, steam pressure, and the footfalls of a giant machine crept closer. The man kicking Slugger froze as Ceteris stared down at him.

"What happened?" asked the hulking off-worlder.

"None of your fuckin' business, alien." The man with the injured groin stood up, hands wrapped tightly around his scrotum. Ceteris did not waste time. The Vagantem aimed his frontal focus cannon at the man, and the black hole at the edge of the barrel lit up and began to smoke like a pipe.

"Alien," repeated Ceteris.

"It was him. They were just protecting me," said a zealous

Dixie as she pointed to the warlord, who was slowly crawling away. Ceteris grabbed him and stood him up.

"Come with me, human." There was nothing Slugger could do but follow. He didn't even turn back to smirk.

As they exited the nightclub, a group of armed men were waiting. "Go in and help the wounded!" the leader shouted to his men. A few ran inside. The leader stayed back and glared at Ceteris. "I'll be taking him now," he then said. He wore a large-brimmed cowboy hat, a sheriff's badge on his coat, and a bolo tie with an American eagle clasp.

"No need," Ceteris struggled to state sternly.

"Why is that?"

Ceteris, however, didn't answer, choosing instead to glare back with a star-speckled gaze.

". . . Alright then, just thought you might need some help," said the sheriff suspiciously. He watched the two until he lost sight of them in the crowds.

The streets crawled with large radioactive rats scurrying in and out of their broken underworld, down sewers and basements and through massive piles of trash and rubble. Slugger watched them stalk the shadows as he passed by, impressed by their organized groups and almost fearless nature. Suddenly, he caught the sight of a cat, orange and mangy, with an eye patch fastened on tightly and carefully. It pounced on a rat and began to tear its entrails out. The surrounding rats, not much smaller than the cat itself, hissed and gnawed the air until the feline's clowder rallied behind it. The rats then retreated to the darkness—for now—though their war with the felines would continue to wage. The warlord remained quiet until they reached the black prison.

"What is your name, human?"

"Slugger," said the warlord bitterly.

"Slogger."

Slugger felt numb, ready to lose. He looked at Ceteris, jealous of his stature and his power, then trudged with a hanging head, reluctant, watching the floor pass by underneath him. As they entered, the many Vagantem eyed the human; this place was not for his kind. The warlord was suddenly confused. Their bare, unsuited forms were a contradiction to his previous notion of them. He looked back at Ceteris and could almost see the weak and frail body underneath.

As they moved down darker and darker hallways, Slugger found himself blinded by the pitch-black, though he was guided by Ceteris's massive steps. An eternity passed by before they reached their supposed destination. The last guard quickly kneeled, waited for Ceteris's permission to rise, then disappeared. The interaction intrigued the warlord.

"This is the human," announced Ceteris to a seemingly empty pit, and in a tongue unrecognizable to Slugger.

"What is this one called?" asked the harsh voice of the prisoner.

"Slogger," said Ceteris, and this word, though hard to distinguish, Slugger understood. There was no Vagantem word for his name.

"I see. Hello, Slogger. I am Nes Bossvan." The prisoner's English was surprisingly clean and comprehendible, yet there was an unfamiliar accent. The warlord had nothing to say; he was frozen, while his mind raced. "You are quite safe here. I assure you."

"Why . . . am I here?" Slugger asked. Rings clicked along the bars of the cell.

"Why are you here is a good question. Perhaps you can enlighten us?" said the prisoner politely. Slugger said nothing, again. "What is your big plan, little human?"

"He does not trust us," argued Ceteris in his true tongue.

"Perhaps. He might need some dark to think on," whispered the prisoner. *"Get some rest, General."*

Slugger was handcuffed to the prisoner's bars, but on the outside of the cell. Heavy steps trailed off and the suit's intricate sounds with them; Ceteris was gone, and Slugger was blind and alone. The prisoner said nothing for a few hours; all the warlord could hear were the occasional scrapes and taps of metal rings.

"What do you want from me?" Slugger eventually found himself asking the dark.

There was a long, bleak silence before a response. "I want many things, human . . . many things for my people."

"Why are you here?" the warlord asked, crippled by his frustration.

"Because I was betrayed. Because we were all betrayed. Lied to, left out . . . used. We lost our world long before you lost yours . . . and we have been chasing something, a new home, ever since. The current leadership believes this to be that new home. Many Vagantem find it unethical, see it as thievery, myself included," said the prisoner.

"Who are you?" Slugger persisted; he was starting to believe this was no ordinary prisoner.

"I am the star teller, the true star teller. I have been usurped and this false king wishes to rule us both. He will only spoil this planet, and our people will slowly rot away until no culture is left, until we are all a soulless amalgamation . . . a society of slaves and little values."

Something clicked inside the warlord's paranoia, and his instincts tickled his bones. He ran through a plethora of possibilities. Why . . . why him, why on earth would they be talking to him? Were they recruiting humans in the city? No. That didn't seem right. Then the fear drained his blood and paled his skin. The canyon; they knew of it somehow. They must know. "Why me?" he asked.

"You are planning something as well . . . are you not?" this time, the prisoner's words were cold.

"Yes, I am." The cogs in the warlord's dark mind began to turn once again.

"I have seen a castle of rock and sand and metal . . . built by humans, many humans," the prisoner revealed. Slugger remained quiet; his fears answered. "Such feats you have accomplished, and without the shield of society. Your leader must be quite competent." The warlord smirked at this.

"He is."

"Can you give word to him? From Nes Bossvan, the true star teller. My offer is this: help me retake my position, dispose of this traitor, and I will make sure to leave your world; to give it back and never return." Despite the thoughts churning, Slugger didn't have much to say, still unsure of himself and this creature's motives. He would not be a pawn. "Others are already on their way, we know of this too. They near the farm," the alien then whispered. The warlord's cards had been revealed, but those who knew were keeping it secret, and suspicion took hold once again.

"How many days have I been here?"

"You were brought by Ceteris to this city close to an Earth's week ago," answered Nes.

"I need to get out of this prison," muttered Slugger.

"We are all prisoners. Remember this . . . when you are outside."

Chapter X – The Great Snake

The Huntress waited outside the black prison. She was steamed and annoyed. Ceteris was by her side. "He was our responsibility. I did not want this incident to reflect on you," the alien explained.

"Still doesn't explain why you brought him here instead of Fox Rivers." She did not give him a glance; instead, she watched all who exited and entered. There were no humans until Slugger finally exited, shading his eyes from the blistering sun. His lips and nose were crusty and chapped, and his clothes seemed pulled and ripped. "Hey!" she called him over.

Slugger had an eerie smile plastered on his face. Ceteris and the Huntress both stared at him, intrigued. "Hey guys," he said with a strange politeness.

"Couldn't stay out of trouble for one night, huh?" she asked sharply.

"I did have fun, though," he said. Ceteris was blank; his thoughts and true feelings unreadable. The Huntress lifted a brow at the smug madman before cracking a smirk.

"Well, you're lucky you didn't kill him, or you'd probably be locked up for good. Now . . . it's time to see what this place is really all about. Come on, since Ceteris bailed on me," said the Huntress as she turned and walked off. Ceteris remained, settling a black eye speckled with white on the warlord before turning around and heading inside the prison. Slugger watched him leave, his heart picking up then slowing, feeling a mixture of doubt and wonder. He then caught up to the Huntress.

Daytime in the city seemed just as busy and reckless as the hours of darkness, and it was a wonder when anyone slept. The sounds were so constant, it was almost numbing to the ear; city silence they called it. Multiple aircrafts passed overhead, and Slugger refused to let himself admire them, but he noticed the Huntress would, when a ship was big and slow enough.

She caught him looking and turned to face him, and a weird jolt of awkwardness shot through his body. She noticed but ignored it. "I probably should have waited for you, but your boy had his first fight. And it'll probably be his last," said the Huntress. Slugger glared at her but soon saw nothing before him, only Ben.

"What happened?" he asked.

The Huntress smiled, wicked and wild. "Are you scared for him?"

"What happened?" he asked again with even less patience.

She sketched his frightened features in her mind before speaking again. "He was unchallenged; his creepy muteness and unnatural size scared all the respected fighters away. All except one. His name was Brutus. Brutus never lost a fight . . . not one. This was a man obsessed with battle; a man who honored all those he put an end to. Your boy was a godsend to him, an opponent finally worthy, or so he proclaimed. The fight was short. It ended so quickly that no one knew what really happened until the body was examined."

The warlord's brow began to sweat, yet he felt cold inside, like a sharp wind was pulling him apart. His sightless eyes trembled, and the Huntress lapped it all up like a cat licks blood. He looked over at her and felt an inexplicable calm, then he smiled back. "You fuckin' . . . you're fuckin' toying with me, aren't you?" She just kept smiling. "You fuckin—"

"Fuckin' what?" she asked, her lip still twisted.

"Fuckin' . . . bitch."

She laughed, and Slugger did not know why.

As she wiped a tear from her cheek, she explained, "Your boy snapped his neck . . . then he killed a referee." The warlord's calm faded and concern arose. "He's no longer allowed in the ring."

"I could have controlled him better," said Slugger tempestuously.

"Yup, probably, but oh well." The Huntress's regret was limited, and now at the end of this conversation, she had completely moved on. "I still won some pebs."

"Where is he?"

"They're keeping him at the ring. The local cops are doing an investigation, but it's just for show, he's in the clear. He is no longer his own man though, if he ever was. You'll need to pick him up and be responsible for him. The Vagantem have their starry eyes on him as well. If he does anything, you'll both be punished like you're one person. Understand?" The warlord nodded. "You're lucky you got friends in Ceteris and I."

As they walked through crowds and huddled buildings, she explained how the city came to be. How a community came together and erected an entirely independent electrical system. And how the Vagantem noticed and offered help. Then one day, once everything was ready, the man behind the idea was found strangled in an alley. The murder remains a mystery, further clouded by passing time and emerging stories.

Slugger thought on this; a man who brought back civilization, only to be left dead and forgotten. The Huntress only vaguely knew of the story, and couldn't even recall the man's name. This angered the warlord, and worried him.

"Hey . . . Huntress!" A voice slightly familiar to the warlord and painfully recognizable to the Huntress called out. She turned with a furious glare. It was the sheriff, and he was alone. He removed his cowboy hat in a respectful manner when he approached. "Howdy," he greeted with a smile that irked the Huntress.

"What do you want, Guy?" she asked with boiling calm.

"Well, besides giving you a greetin', I actually came for him." The sheriff then directed his attention toward Slugger, who stared back blankly. The Huntress ground her molars.

"Why?"

"I hope I'm not interrupting anything special, but this is the man who killed the poachers . . . is he not?" The sheriff's grin was cruel and chill-delivering.

"He's clear," snapped the Huntress.

"Not by me. I got some questions."

"If you want to know more, go to the ID center and read up, it's all there. They cleared him, we checked his story and everything."

"Well . . ." began the sheriff as he fitted his cowboy hat back on, "it's one thing when killing in self-defense in a sticky situation, especially out there. But your boy caused some more trouble last night. Gotta make sure this isn't a recurring thing."

"He won't from here on out . . . I promise. My name is all over this asshole's docs, I'll be in as much shit as him if he keeps this up. Now," she rested her hand gently on his arm, "don't be jealous. I'm just showing him the best of this place, getting him familiar." She then lightly tapped his chin before shoving him back. "Now fuck off already, Sheriff. I got this under control." Her wink secured his decision and put a smile on his face.

"Oh, cold lady of winter, dark mistress of my tortured heart. I will be seeing you again, and you as well . . . Slugger." The sheriff turned and began singing an old love song.

Eventually, they reached the Blake-Shire Bowl. A constant stream of people swarmed in through the main entrance. Traders were all over, blabbering almost unintelligibly about their next deal. The Huntress, however, directed Slugger toward the VIP box. Past the gate and the door with the Native American knocker, the thin, pierced woman greeted them with a wicked smile.

"Treat him to whatever, but—" The Huntress put her bony hand on his shoulder and pinched, then glared at him. "Do not get into any trouble this time . . . okay?" Slugger was already smiling, and he gave her a nod of compliance.

Slugger sat behind the cracked glass pane that looked over the arena. This time, it was not a desert, but an artificial jungle striped with an array of colors and pierced through by a slender rill, like a murky blue fissure. Behind him, bets were being placed and tedious conversations were had.

"And, how do they do it?"

"Well . . . I don't understand the technology quite yet, but it seems like a very basic process."

"Really?"

"Oh yes. Well, once all the groundwork is laid. So, the previous land is removed except a portion that is purposely seared and mixed in with the new soil. The alien's soil is a strange grey sand and mulch."

"Okay, but how they do it so fast?"

"I'm getting there. They hard pack it, then drop a weird jelly-like substance and spread it all around evenly. They then drop this acid-like substance on top of the jelly, creating a bubbling chemical reaction."

"Hm."

"Then they spray water, or some kind of clear liquid, onto it. Once it's dry, they send their bots to start raking the ground with lasers and lights, sowing the field with seeds and trailing a blue gas."

"Are you serious? And then the environment just sprouts up the next day?"

"Usually longer, but pretty much. Some of the bigger trees and rocks are transported in, though."

This conversation intrigued Slugger until the horns blew and the perimeter of fire tubes belched rainbow flame. The crowds silenced, as did the men and women sitting and talking behind Slugger.

A man entered the arena with his hands up. He had a sky-reaching top hat decorated with the bones of small creatures. His jeans were skintight and the material was torn away at the knees. The man began to flap his blazer like the wings of a black bird. Then he spoke, pulling out a microphone from his jacket's pocket.

"Iiiiiiiiit's fiiiiiiiiight niiiiiight!" he blared over the speakers, and the crowd grew feral. Some climbed onto the chain-link dome while various scuffles broke out in the ensuing chaos. One man smashed his head on the gate as if he was trying to squeeze through the holes. As the band played, the announcer did a backflip, and his hat fell off when he was upside down. Before picking it up, he ran circles in the dirt and kicked his legs out like a cancan dancer.

The drawbridge gate that the beasts of the arena were released through began to rattle and clank. The crowds hushed and the announcer turned anxiously. Suddenly, the Huntress entered from the fighter's side, and the crowd erupted in a frenzy more intense than before. "Let us welcome . . . the Hunter!" blasted the announcer as he grabbed her hand and lifted it as if she were already the victor.

She pulled her hand back and socked the man across the jaw. He fell and spat out blood, though more continued to flow. "The Huntress . . . get it right," she hissed. The man smiled. He stood up, brushed off the dirt, and wiped away some more blood.

"I mean, the Huntress!" he corrected, and the audience continued to be rambunctious.

The announcer exited, jumping up and down and clapping his heels together, as the Huntress focused on the gate her opponent would soon come through. All she knew was its name: the twin snake.

The gate opened up with a deafening and rustic croak. All was silent now—all but the scaly slither of a limbless monster. The trees and plants were soaked with dew, dripping as if it had just rained, and the mud allowed the creature to slide its massive body around with ease. The Huntress watched it enter, then watched it rear a good forty feet high from across the artificial jungle. A pair of large yellow eyes with white slits locked her in place, like Medusa's curse. She stared at it, curious.

There were cancerous scales and tumors, hard as stone, running sporadically down its body. The great snake, over one hundred feet long, was not one beast, but two. Its singular spine split before the necks, and bare, unfinished bone peeked out at the division. The serpent's left head snapped its jaws like a rabid dog and stared down anything that moved. Its eyes were black, almost unseen against its black skin, but on each side of its cobra hood were large false yellow eyes.

The second head, off to the right, seemed docile and unintelligent. The creature's eyes were white, small, and beady; they seemed unseeing. Its jaws remained open and crooked, almost as if it had been broken and healed inefficiently. A pale drool, sparkling like glitter, slowly trickled down, and steam rose from the puddle; it was acidic, eating away at the ground. The head would have seemed paralyzed or dead if the tongue didn't peek out and flicker every so often. Unlike its twin, this head did not have the hood of a cobra, but rather a sharp horn atop its nose. The left head sent a screeching hiss, originating from the depths of hell, that threatened the world and scraped the scalps of all within an earshot.

The Huntress yanked her scarf off and began blotting her sweat-drenched face and neck in a vain attempt to battle the humidity. The creature began to creep its way over; her time was counting down. She took a last look at the snake and smiled before running toward the trees, recalling the priest's tactic of striking from above. At the rill's bank was a tree that seemed inverted; the branches were short toward the base but got longer at the top, it sprouted rounded fans of autumn leaves, and its bark was grey with descending swirls of light brown. It was twisted and bent at the low end, but straightened out at the top.

She rushed her way higher and higher up the tree until she slipped and lost her balance. She was able to catch herself but was forced to watch her spear stab the ground after its drop. Now unarmed, she looked for her foe. In the struggle up the massive tree, she had managed to lose the two-headed serpent. Despite its lumbering size, it was quiet, patient, and calculating. The jungle was a miniature recreation of the twin snake's true home. The green and black of the scales hadn't seemed like the right colors to blend in with the surroundings, but it was gone, nonetheless.

Some of the audience yelled and pointed, but to no avail. The Huntress would not shift her focus, not this time. Then the wood tremored, and she realized that the snake was constricting around the base of the tree. Loud snaps and splintering sent the Huntress into a panic. She narrowed her eyes and saw movement below. The snake was no longer green and black, but toned in autumn colors, and she stared as the tree began to sway. She tried to jump from the tree's pinnacle, but got caught on a snagging branch, pulling her back as it fell in the opposite direction.

The tree hit the ground, the impact softened by the grass bedding and mulch. It flicked the Huntress off like a trebuchet. She flew through the air briefly before slamming down upon pulsating flesh, hard and scaled over. The snake was tangled up in the collapsed tree, and the left head seemed to blame the right. The woman slipped through a loop in the snake's body and moved away from the creature. She was limping; her foot felt broken and cold, and her shoe was filling with blood. The serpent's heads refocused and watched the injured woman attempting to run before darting after her.

The Huntress desperately limped toward her spear, which was still stuck in the ground. She pulled it out and held it firmly just as the twin snake reached her. The woman, hardened by years of fear and danger, lost all thought and acted on pure instinct. She chucked the spear straight and precise, and the pike miraculously struck the exposed spinal cord at the head's split.

The left head shrieked as its hood drooped. The right head seemed to be in pain as well, but its motions were limited. The left head suddenly bit into its twin and ended its life. As the creature's jaws let go, the fangs and tongue of the left head began steaming as if corroding. The left began to shriek even more while whipping its head and body around. The Huntress was able to crawl away toward the gladiator's entrance, leaving a bloody trail.

Slugger got up and left, while those around him chattered with worry or disappointment. Before leaving, he was met by the pierced woman. "Worried about your friend?" she asked. The warlord wasn't all that worried, but he nodded nonetheless. "She'll be okay," she said. Slugger nodded again in quiet agreement, caring little either way.

"May I see some of the other creatures?" he could not help but to ask; he needed to see. The woman stretched an ugly smile.

"There are four holding centers, and each can be visited for the right price. The closest one holds the biggest beasts, while the others go down in size. Look for Odyssey Sun Zoo and Aquarium, over by the airport. It's no secret where they are, but getting an actual peek inside, again, will cost you."

Slugger's smile was unreadable, but the pierced woman, used to a strange crowd, thought little of it. "Thank you," he said. The warlord turned but stopped before taking another step. The pierced woman observed this patiently, awaiting more questions. "Where's the fighting ring?" he asked.

The woman chuckled. "The Bowl beats the fighting ring any day."

Slugger did not respond and just stared emptily at her, awaiting his answer. The woman then grew annoyed. "Go on! Find it yourself. I'm not a fucking map." Slugger's half smile lifted on one side, then he was gone.

Slugger wandered late into the night, mapping the city into his mind. He spoke with many locals, as he had much to discover, but he kept his motives concealed. His final stop was the black prison. Ceteris was by the entrance, arguing with the two guards stationed there.

The guards suddenly stopped conversing and watched the strange human approach. Ceteris turned, and his eyes blackened as they met the warlord's. "What are you doing here, human?"

"I came to find you," said Slugger. The three Vagantem remained silent and staring, waiting for more. Slugger looked at each of their faces, protected by their clear bubble-like helmets. The aliens inside the suits were all slightly different shades. Ceteris was grey, and the other two were differing blues. "The Huntress, she's hurt."

"Where . . . is she?" asked Ceteris, almost confused.

"Where do you think?" spat the warlord with an eerie smile. Ceteris's eyes began to speckle with stars. "She'll be fine, probably. Just thought I'd tell you." It seemed to the Vagantem that Slugger was taunting him; that he was at least enjoying himself in the reveal. "May I speak to him?" he then asked.

Ceteris stared back, analyzing this creature before him, then he looked back at the guards. "Him," Ceteris repeated. "No." He then grabbed the warlord by the arm and pulled him a short distance away. The metal grasp was crushing and cold, and the bullet wound in Slugger's shoulder began to feel stretched and beaten.

"What the fuck!" shouted the warlord.

"Silence," answered the Vagantem. Once they stopped and Ceteris was satisfied with the lonesome alley he had pulled the warlord into, he spoke, struggling to be stern with his gauche human speech. "Your men are approaching the farm. I think it is time for you to make your move." Ceteris's starry eyes were haunting, like black lagoons reflecting the night sky. Slugger felt slightly shell-shocked from the gaze alone.

"My move?" he asked as if he had just woken from an ancient slumber. Ceteris remained patient. He had watched the warlord closely, and at the same time monitored the canyon base and the army of survivors who dwelled there. For days he had followed groups moving in and out and found outposts scattered throughout the unexplored land. Now, his wing was following this incoming group, and he was beginning to see a blossoming potential greater than his brother's mere escape.

"Let me see the marking on yorm?" asked Ceteris.

Slugger stared back with lips twitching upward; he almost wanted to point and laugh. "Yorm?"

"Your . . . arm," the alien corrected. Under a stifled chuckle, the warlord lifted his sleeve and revealed his new tattoo. Ceteris studied it, and Slugger studied him. Suddenly, a hot click came from the barrel of Ceteris's frontal focus cannon, and it began to whistle and screech like two slabs of metal sliding against each other. The black hole began to light up like a soft pink jewel; it wasn't a laser red like it had been when he threatened the men in the night club. "This will hurt," the alien said as he firmly grabbed hold of the warlord once again.

Suddenly, a pink needle of light shot out and began to burn away the top layer of skin from Slugger's arm. The black and blue ink of the tattoo was erased, but Ceteris continued, and

Slugger endured.

The warlord was wincing and cringing and his eyes dried as they bulged and pulsed almost outside his skull. "Fuuuuuuck!" he shouted, but it was another several excruciating moments before the Vagantem finished his work. The pink light needle retracted, and the strenuous sounds of machinery silenced.

"Make sure to burn your friend's marking as well," Ceteris told him. "They will be able to find you if you don't." Suddenly, he was off.

The warrior clicked and clanked through the crowds with his sunmetal armor and vanished behind a screen of dark and smoke. Slugger did not watch him leave; his eyes were stuck on the ground. A used condom, a dead rat, and a deflated baby doll lay there. The guards before the black prison glared at the human in both pity and disgust as he passed.

Slugger wandered again, trying to slow and ease his thoughts. He contemplated getting on a bus at its stop, but there were too many people for his liking. The fighting ring was on the opposite side of the city, and he was told it would take at least two hours on foot to reach it. His shoes were cheap and held together poorly; he missed his boots. Something pushed him forward, as something always did. Whether that was fear, curiosity, or revenge, he was unsure, but self-preservation was an all-encompassing layer; a driving force behind all avenues of his decision-making process. He suddenly came across a familiar sight: a small government building guarded by spiked rails and barbed wire. On each side were large apartment complexes comprised of rotting and discolored brick.

A man stalking the streets with a shotgun in hand and a ski mask over his head shouted, "Hey, you!" Slugger turned to face him. There were others crisscrossing through the roads and sidewalks, and the man cut into the flow of people. He laid the sawed-off shotgun over his shoulder when they met. The large bulging eyes almost seemed to jump out of the man's skull. "I heard the Huntress met her match . . . she okay?" asked the man.

Slugger nodded, growing annoyed that he was constantly considered her friend. The man sensed the irritation in the warlord and lifted his brow. "Where are you off to?" he asked. The man brought the sawed-off down from off his shoulder and into his readied hands before pumping it.

"The fighting ring, to find my buddy," said the warlord with a smile. The man did not smile back. "Can you help me?" The man walked away without a response, back toward the entrance gate, and began to dig through a trash bag of supplies piled nearby. When he found the desired item, he returned. It was a map of the city, folded into a tiny square. It was made well before the world's end, but much had been added to it.

"I'd try to catch a bus or carriage . . . shit's pretty far. The stops are marked."

Slugger nodded gratefully. "What about my stuff?"

The man cocked his head. "Not here. It was picked up and claimed already."

Slugger scoffed, and the Huntress's hideous smile consumed his mind. He was off without a word. Unbeknownst to him, a spy was sent to follow.

After some hours rolled by, he finally found the fighting ring. He was tired, hungry, and annoyed; the old familiar stings. The stadium had a perfect spherical cap. Large concrete arches and statues styled its face and welcomed the crowds. Two beams of light shot through the opening like yellow lasers, and it seemed like a big fight had just occurred, as the flow of people was mostly coming out.

Slugger lurked around outside the arena until it was relatively empty. When he entered, he found a group by the ring discussing the recent bets and the riches and losses that had just befallen them. The group was well-dressed in clean and stiff pressed suits. One of them was the quiet man whose gaze had stuck with the warlord when he initially entered the city. Slugger was suddenly reminded how sorrowful and apologetic the man's eyes had been.

Of the group of three that had greeted them upon entry, the quiet man was the only one present; the rest of those gathered by the ring were unfamiliar. Two statues in their shadows turned out to be guards in similarly pressed suits holding on to bright, bulky Vagantem rifles, each etched with strange markings and frilled with opaque dishes by the sharp barrels. Slugger noticed that, although they were still, these men seemed clumsy, or at least awkward, with the alien guns.

"Fight's over!" a fat man shouted as he wiped at the constant beads of sweat forming at the edges of his face. He looked winded and soaked. The others looked then glanced away—all except the one who recognized Slugger.

"I know this one," the man said, and Slugger smirked.

"I've come here for my friend," said the warlord.

"The big one?" asked the man, and Slugger nodded. "Well, you'll have to submit a request." The bushy brows of the warlord trembled and sank. "I'm sure you've come a long way just to find this out," said the man understandingly, "but these are our processes. It is paramount that we abide by them." The rest of the group darted nervous eyes to each other while some turned their backs to the warlord, wanting to get back to their previous discussion.

"I was told I could pick him up, and that I am responsible for him now." Slugger's voice was tight with impatience. The fat man chortled until he was silenced by the warlord's dead eyes.

"Of course; however, they cannot let him out without the proper paperwork. I let you go before, but this is not my jurisdiction. I cannot make the call here," said the familiar man.

"Then who can?" asked Slugger. The fat man raised his hand.

"I make the call, and we must go through the proper channels," pronounced the fat man. His skin was orange and blotchy and his hair was brown and white.

Suddenly, a Vagantem entered, towering over them all. The armor was plated and powered, but there was no large photon turret attached to the shoulder, nor was there a specialized focus cannon situated on the front like the others. The focus cannon was still present, but it was retracted underneath the chest plate. Her facial tentacles were thin and more refined than the males and the gripping pads on the underside were smaller and smoother as well. Behind her transparent bubble-like headwear, her alien skin gleamed a pinkish red.

But what was most striking of all was the way the Vagantem stood and walked. Unlike the hulking and slouching mechs, weighted down by mass and power, this suit straightened the spine and kept the back upright. As a species, the Vagantem's skeletons were more malleable than a human's.

"I sometimes think . . . that the recent imposition of the rule of law has only intensified your thirst for arbitrary rules," she said. Her voice was elegant and crisp, modulated with a tool similar to Ceteris's. The tang of her words was classy and British, and it was apparent where she had mastered her English. The others looked at her, but only the man Slugger knew smiled as she approached.

"Emissary Lenovosm," the familiar man said, bowing low. She rested her metal hand atop his head briefly before he was allowed up again. "How goes you?"

"Always looking behind my back and hoping not to get killed down here; you know, the usual." The others laughed—all but the fat man, who kept his suspicious glare on Slugger.

"Did you see the fight?"

"I'm afraid I missed it. Perhaps next time. I actually came down to see you, Evaluator," she explained. Slugger began to tense. He felt ignored and invisible.

"Hey! Where's my friend!" he growled. The others were startled at his outburst, even the Vagantem emissary. The fat man's orange skin turned red.

"Who do you think you are?" the fat man demanded.

"A new citizen." Slugger felt stupid; he knew he had to play his cards right. He began to cool, forcing deference upon himself. "We have been separated since we arrived. He is . . . not well. He needs me." Slugger's plea was powered by true conviction and a heart that was almost human.

The fat man, blotchy and sweaty, turned to his companion. "He's talking about the big one, yes?" The evaluator nodded. "He killed two men!" he shouted after turning back to face Slugger. "And, if I'm not mistaken, you're the ones who killed the poachers."

"The poachers?" asked the emissary.

"The singers who brought all types of creatures to the Bowl," the friendly evaluator explained.

"Ah . . . yes. I liked them. Especially the quiet one. Poor souls."

"It was in self-defense. None of you know what it's like out there!" Slugger barked.

"I don't know why they let you out, but the big one is too dangerous," the fat man said.

Slugger's gaze fell, thinking, then shot back up. "Yes. I told the Huntress he was not ready to fight. And I told her I needed to see him or else something like this would happen. She didn't believe me, and look how it turned out." The small crowd grew silent. "Did she not share that this man is completely and blindly loyal to me? That he'd do anything I asked? We were forced here, tied together and left sitting in our own piss and shit, hungry and thirsty every day. No one gave me a chance!"

The group listened and looked at each other in disbelief from time to time. The emissary, however, did not take her eyes off Slugger, this filthy and erratic man who made her feel privileged and ashamed. She raised her hand to stop him.

"Please, we have heard enough," she said. Slugger bore his sights straight through her, and although she felt this, she did not falter. "I have only just started visiting planetside. I am new to this city. This is supposed to be a place for all lost humans; to give them a chance at society again." The Vagantem then trailed off, looking into the view of the star-flecked sky through the exit's grand doorway. "My whole life, I saw out a window from inside the hull of a ship. I complained, and sulked, then grew bored." She inhaled deeply and it whistled through her metal armor. "Maybe I didn't have it so bad."

This made the back of Slugger's throat dry with a stinging itch. He cleared it awkwardly. His admission of helplessness was sickening; it made him want to close his eyes, or hurt someone. But he also felt lighter and less pressed; even freer.

"Let him out, and keep an extra eye on him," said the emissary as her facial tentacles danced with a liberating delight and her eyes filled with stars.

"But the paperwork?" retorted the fat man, not so conflicted as the rest. Slugger slapped himself with an open palm and pulled down, stretching his skin downward as if to yank his own face off in annoyance.

"What is with all this paperwork?" the warlord asked, as he tried to calm himself yet again.

"Everyone's profile is compiled with any and all data pertaining to that person. Those who have reached star-class citizenship will be able to apply to live on the moon base," the fat man explained, dignified.

"That is moon-class. Star-class is fleetside." The emissary corrected him.

Slugger chuckled, forgetting the words just as he heard them. He was on the verge of snapping; he couldn't afford any more distractions. He must proceed, but with patience, and charm. "Don't worry, one day you'll be worthy I'm sure," he said. The others joined in a laugh.

"How dare you! I am allowed up there any time I please," yapped the fat man.

"Well, that's just not true," said a member of the group.

"Shut it!" he belched back.

Suddenly, before anyone even saw him move, Slugger was resting his icy hand upon the fat man, who stood much shorter than him. They locked eyes, and the fat man's sweat intensified.

"Please, just give me a break." The warlord's voice had no emotion. The fat man snorted. "What if I . . ." Slugger caught himself. "Can I speak with you privately, for just a moment?" The fat man stared, annoyed yet curious.

"You," the fat man pointed at one of the guards. "Follow me." The group moved on to a new discussion while Slugger, the fat man, and the guard wandered off to the side. "What is it?" the man demanded.

"I have some pebbles," Slugger revealed. The fat man's eyes grew hungry, like black holes.

"This is not a cheap favor." Slugger ruffled through his pockets until he found the five pebbles, each catching the light like open lakes. When he showed them, the fat man snorted again, like a stubborn pig. "This your whore money? This looks like only a few hours' worth."

"This is all I have," pleaded Slugger.

"Fine!" The fat man pouted, snatching the currency. They headed back toward the ring, and the fat man then reached for a document on the judges' table. He signed a dotted line toward the bottom. "Fill this in, get the warden's signature, and make sure to bring it back sometime this week." Slugger lifted his half smile. "I mean it! I am already making a note of it and we will come looking for you if need be." The searing pain of his burnt forearm was suddenly noticeable, and he knew why. They could go looking for him all they wanted, but now they wouldn't be able to track him.

The evaluator patted the fat man's back. "I guess you're not a total asshole," the evaluator chided. The fat man shoved his arm away.

* * *

There was a police station that housed inmates a few blocks from the arena. There were a few jails scattered out around the city, but this was the closest and most fortified. The main door opened and poured white light all over the black asphalt, lifting the surrounding dark. A ring of several armed men emerged from the white, each with golden star badges to denote their authority. A Vagantem warrior stomped the ground behind them. In the middle of them all was a shaggy beast, a giant man whose steps and breaths were silent. It was Big Ben, but he seemed slightly different from when Slugger had seen him last.

Slugger eyed him, cocking his head slowly. The old chains at his wrists, once embedded into his skin, had been removed and replaced. A long waist chain connected his wrists to his sides and prevented a longer stride by locking at the ankles. He had a new marking on his arm, as Slugger did, stamped with black ink. There were also newly stitched lacerations all over his body, brighter than his old scars. His hair lay matted and thick, shining as if wet but cold and parched. Dry blood caked his ear and forehead. Ben looked down; he usually looked down upon most, but this time, his sight was glued to the ground. This angered the warlord, but his smile stayed. So close, he thought; almost there.

"Thank you, my good sirs. Now please, unlock my friend and we will be on our way, continuing in our efforts to be perfect citizens." Even Slugger found that too much and he hushed, refusing to say any more or let further sarcasm seep out. Ben was still as he was released, eyes still locked on the ground.

The Vagantem behind him shoved him forward once he was unchained, but the giant quickly caught his footing. His head remained lowered, even as his master and long companion patted him on his bare back. Slugger heard the word freak being whispered from the group, and he silently agreed. They were both freaks. But they were also powerful men, and patient.

Just down the block, the pair was intercepted by a drone with twin gyroscopic propellers and a set of three blue light eyes arranged in a triangle behind clear plating. The device was small, the size of a human head. The warlord jumped. "What the fuck?"

"The fuck . . ." repeated a voice from the drone. "It is Ceteris. I would like to talk."

Chapter XI – Rupture

The Huntress awoke the next morning with a cold rag upon her forehead. She felt heavy with confusion and dazed from the drugs. Looking around, she realized she was home, and she immediately panicked. "Peas!" she shouted after blowing a few kisses out into the air. Her cat did not reply. "Peas!"

"Huntress." Ceteris's voice made the glass tremble. She looked out and saw the Vagantem standing outside, staring at her through an open window. She rubbed her eyes, and as she tried to get out of bed, found a thick cast holding her foot. Her back and arms felt sore, and she could feel a new gash under her chin.

"Where's my cat?" she asked.

"Cat . . . I do not know what that is."

"You probably scared her. Did you come in the house?"

"I could not fit. I had some of the nurses from the hospital bring you here and lay you down," Ceteris said.

"Peas!" she called again. The Huntress finally escaped her sheets, and she searched while Ceteris waited patiently outside. "There you are," she said affectionately after spotting the cat squeezed into a niche between the fridge and cabinets. Her attitude lightened as she strolled over to her window, now ready to talk to her Vagantem friend, stomping and thudding with her cast. "What happened? Did you see my fight?" she asked, speaking through the window, still in a slight daze.

"I was unable to. Slogger told me about your condition," said Ceteris.

She giggled. "I don't think it was Slogger." Ceteris remained quiet, blinking distractedly. "Where is he?"

"He's with me," informed Ceteris as he looked out and motioned with his arm, as if signaling to approach. The Huntress could tell the Vagantem was slightly removed from their conversation.

"Let him in."

Slugger walked in with a yellow smile and a rotten stench. Ben remained outside, silent by the alien warrior that towered over even him, still looking down.

"My lady," he said as he bowed. The Huntress furrowed her brows.

"What'd you think of the fight?" She seemed a little too hungry for the answer, even for

Slugger.

"Well . . . to be completely honest, it was fuckin' awesome," he lied. "I loved every second of it," he lied again. "You . . . seriously are scary." This time, he spoke the truth. The Huntress plastered a wicked smirk across her face. Her whole life, she had felt she needed to prove herself. Despite the prestige she already enjoyed, it would never be enough.

"Seems like you two reunited," the Huntress said as she glanced at the giant outside her house. Slugger nodded with a fake pleasure. "What is it?" she suddenly asked.

"Hmm?"

"I seriously doubt you came all this way to check on little old me. Am I right?"

Slugger shrugged.

"What do you want?" she pressed.

"Our stuff," the warlord demanded.

"Right, right. You'll find two duffle bags in the guest room. Everything in there is yours. Touch anything else, and I'll take your fuckin' hand," she threatened as she slowly crawled back into bed.

Slugger darted down the hall. The two duffle bags sprawled across an empty room made his mouth water and his left eye faintly twitch. There were his blades, his silent sisters, safely sheathed inside his belt. His knife-toed boots awaited him as well. He cradled them before donning both. Ben's mace was also there, which was almost all he had taken with him.

"Where's the rifle?" Slugger asked sharply.

"Over the fireplace; but you're not taking that," shot the Huntress.

"Oh, no?" The warlord begged to differ as he looked up to see it mounted on a trophy stand. The Huntress only grinned wickedly, her eyes burning. Slugger paled, and his eyes seemed to go hollow and soulless. "I see . . . come on big guy, let's get the fuck out of this hellhole."

The Huntress was taken aback as she watched the two take off without any farewell. "Guess I really dropped the ball on those two," she said.

"The ball," Ceteris repeated.

"Might have to pay a little visit to the farmer," she said more thoughtfully.

"Huntress." She looked up at the Vagantem to find his face darkened, as if the clouds in his thoughts were real and present. "There is something I must ask of you."

* * *

The warlord wasted no time in leaving the city. He felt more hateful than ever, but aimless as well. The city sentries let him by, thinking nothing of it, and thinking they could always track him if need be. They took the same path they had entered from: past the welcoming arches and to the raised freeway, where they met the trio colonies of the mist spores. On foot, they were much more able to step carefully to avoid setting off the powdered miasmas. Daylight was descending and Slugger was at his peak anxiety.

Where was his approaching party; which men had Brody gathered? What was his next move? "In three days, look for the eye of blood, high in the sky," Ceteris had said to him before they'd arrived at the Huntress's home from the hospital. Why did he speak like they were coconspirators? Why did he act like they had grand plans behind the scenes? He hadn't even accepted the alien's eerie proposition. Perhaps in the long-term, they could prove to be valuable allies; the potential flowered in his mind. Through this Vagantem power struggle, he could be the one to permanently remove them from his world.

Still, all Slugger wanted to do for now was escape, lick the freedom in the air, and return to his home, where the canyon was, where the Lost Boys were near, and where Marge looked at him, so stupid and docile. Then he thought of Homer and lost himself in the empty sockets of the creature's skeletal image standing before him. It then vanished and he blinked, dumbfounded. Nothing but a cruel mirage playing tricks on him again.

The Bowl, the Blake-Shire Bowl; that is where they had planned to take Homer, to play with him, to laugh and cheer at his death. "No," whispered the warlord. Everything seemed to be lined up; he knew what he was going to do. Not for him or Nes, but for Homer . . . for Marge. The floral tunnel began to form up ahead; first sparsely green, then rainbowed with flowers. Time passed with Slugger lost in thought, and the farmer's orchard eventually poked up above the horizon.

Slugger paused, lifting his hand for Ben to do the same. They studied the distance, wondering where the farmer's snipers were. He watched, reluctant. Wasn't he a free citizen? What could the farmer do to him now?

They pressed on and made it through the strange orchard of trees, both earthly and otherworldly. Silence suddenly engulfed them. Nothing, not even an insect buzz or wind, brushed their ears. They crept closer, toward the porch of the farmhouse where the farmer would sit and smoke on his rocking chair.

Nothing.

There was no blood, no body, no sign of anything. They searched the barn and found nothing, then went back to the porch to think. Slugger sat on the steps, elbows digging into his knees and chin resting on his clasped knuckles. The creatures seemed spooked and shaken up; even the black cattleworms, whose emotions were hard to read. The cows and swine had fled to the other side of their pen whenever the two got close. Something had happened here, and it had been concealed. A smile stretched his face.

Almost an hour had passed when an ear-piercing shot cracked the silence. Then a shadowy group of individuals revealed themselves from the direction of the ridge. "What was that?" said the warlord as they approached, numbly unalarmed.

"You were being followed," said a sniper with bushy brows and a weak chin.

"Was it a woman?" asked the warlord. He shook his head, and Slugger was almost relieved. "Has it been fourteen days already?"

"Just about," said a man with a wilting mohawk. He had a large knife sheathed and hanging from a piece of rope around his neck.

"Thanks, Brody." The warlord eyed each man, taking account. "Don, Cass, Noodle, Bashar, Lonnie, Bones, Johnson, Moose, Rats, Pyro, Michael, Kraven, Ren, Striker, Dinesh, Trolley, Canada, Stew, Duke, Foreskin, Jacob, Tech, Guts, and Java," his tone hardened, and he suddenly remembered how to be a leader again. "You were brought here for an important task. Quite possibly the most important mission to date. Did Brody or any of the returners share any details with you?" asked the warlord.

"I mentioned we found something, and that there might be a big group out here," answered Brody.

"And you?" asked the warlord, directing his question to the surgeon and the other returners.

Canada shook his head. "No point. They're already out here, might as well hear it from you."

"I had to kill Greg," Brody blurted. His voice was hollow and remorseless. Slugger lifted a brow. "He returned with the initial group and refused to come back with me. He handed the map over and said we'd have to kill him if we wanted to stop him from headin' home. So I did, and threw him down the crack."

Slugger nodded. "Atta boy. What'd you do with the farmer and his men?"

"Disposed of 'em. Chopped them up and fed 'em to the critters," interrupted Moose, a lanky gentleman who still wore a pair of shades in spite of the dark. The warlord chuckled wildly.

"What're your orders, Boss?" asked the sniper, Java. "We came ready."

Respect. He almost didn't recognize it. "Three days . . ." he spat eerily.

"And then?"

"And then the fun begins."

* * *

In the deep black of isolation, caged and chained against walls of shadow, Nes Bossvan stirred. Like a gator's eyes floating above the water, he waited. The chain's grip restricted him, and he was always in pain. Suddenly, the thunderous steps of Ceteris sang hope into his muddled mind. *"Prime General?"* he muttered in his native tongue.

"I am no general," the warrior replied.

"This argument grows tiresome. Yes, you are."

"Rada and Pax are here," said Ceteris softly.

"And the warden?" asked Nes.

"He is with us. But he must not seem so. He will act contrary, even when none are seemingly around, to hide this fact. We must trust him."

"No. We must watch him. He is no friend to Auroron, but he is no friend to us either," warned the prisoner sternly.

"We need him."

"For now. When will I see Rada and Pax?" asked Nes.

"Tomorrow, on the day of the blood moon," confirmed Ceteris.

"Blood moon," Nes scoffed. *"And what of this escort?"*

Ceteris remained silent, as if mourning a previous hope. *"She has refused me. We must find another way."*

"Refused you? And now she wanders, knowing parts of our plan?"

"The Huntress will never betray me," blasted Ceteris.

"She is human. Why would she care?" Ceteris remained silent. *"Do you know why I'm here? Why he chose to trap me on this godless rock? Because he thought I belonged with them. He wants me to watch them scurry around, pretend they are not a dead race, treat them as if they had traversed the stars like us. They are feral . . . all of them. Worse even than the Critori, who shared our sun."*

"They can be of use," said Ceteris, though Nes continued as if he did not hear this.

"He made sure none could visit or speak with me. That spineless pool swimmer. He wants to erase me. To pretend I do not exist."

"I came," Ceteris said softly.

"Yes, you did. Because you are a true prime general. Because you could never abandon your star teller. Because you remembered: we are brothers. And then they stripped you of everything."

"We will get it all back," assured Ceteris.

"Yes . . . what of the other human?"

"I . . . I told him to make a distraction on the night of the blood moon." Ceteris was doubtful.

"And?" hissed Nes.

"To speak true, I have little faith in him. I torched the markings on the two and vaporized their tracker beads. If they chose to, they could leave and never return. I recalled my wing to the city. They have no reason to come back. I might have . . . dropped ball."

"Dropped ball, what is this?"

"A human saying," said Ceteris, and then he heard the agitated writhing of Vagantem tentacles and the scrape of rings.

"What was your plan?" Nes's tone was harsher than usual, stressed for the coming day.

"I did not want the others to find him if he decides to make his move. I saw death in his eyes . . . a vile bloodthirst. He is destruction, as is the root of all beings."

"Human beings," corrected Nes. *"How do you see your own people?"*

Ceteris ignored this. *"There is a chance he will come back on the day I told him. The group that followed him were prepared for something."*

"You've spent too long with humans. We still have allies, true allies," said Nes.

"None, though, who dare to take you from this rock and hide you among the fleet," Ceteris pointed out. *"Maybe whispered prayers and secret promises hold you over, but not me."* Ceteris sounded impatient.

"They cannot reveal themselves yet. Do you think that would be wise? To come and start a war without moving everything in place first? You are a general, are you not?"

"These politics are insufferable," foamed Ceteris.

"What about Pax and Rada? Perhaps they could assist in providing refuge as well?" Nes suggested thoughtfully.

"They are already being watched for coming down here. He would expect us to hide with them."

"Were they not careful?" asked Nes.

"They were smuggled in by remnants of the Commerce Guild . . . but the guild warned of spies, and a deepening split between Old Ones and the Auroron loyalists among them. They managed to pass the barrier with no trouble, however, word will surely get back to him."

"I see." A terrible silence broke out, like a storm cloud brewing in the distance; then Nes spoke again. *"I'm formulating a plan. I think I now know what to do."*

Chapter XII – Under the Blood Moon

The night was late and the sky was black, blotched with grey clouds. Stars flecked the endless scape. The moon was full of blood, red like a heart released from its chest, still throbbing. Its warm, murderous color boiled above the dim dusk, glowing sadly. It was maddening. It was engulfing.

The city life seemed undisturbed; raucous and normal. The people were distracted and cold. The identification center was busy, with citizens in and out of the facility. The man in the ski mask was having a conversation over the radio. "Have you heard from Stiller yet?"

"No, sir. The two were said to have left through the archway."

"When and where did they go?"

"Not sure. Stiller told the sentries he was following them. I was waitin' for more details, but they haven't responded in over an hour." The voice behind the radio was reluctant and nervous.

"An hour? Go and check on them! And send someone over to the Huntress to get some answers. Wait . . . I gotta go. Check on them, and talk to the Huntress!"

"Yes, sir."

"Emissary!" shouted the man in the ski mask.

A tall and slender Vagantem in armor turned to reply. "Yes?"

"As security manager, I must stay with you until you leave. To ensure your safety," said the man nervously.

"Then keep up, will you? I am very busy, and keep that thing lowered!" she snapped. The security officer removed his sawed-off shotgun from over his shoulder and gripped it firmly while the barrel eyed the ground. They moved to a lone office and entered. "I'm getting quite sick of your cumbersome gravity," she complained.

The pair's brief discussion regarding document and data storage was interrupted by a series of bombs exploding in unison outside, like bells from the underworld. On the floor below them, gunfire erupted. The security manager pumped his shotgun and dashed for the door.

"Wait! You're supposed to protect me!" Emissary Lenovosm shouted after him, but it was too late; he was gone. She looked outside the window and saw several pillars of fire and smoke on the horizon. Vagantem drones and sirens crisscrossed the chaos. People were screaming and running. Animals of all kinds were on the loose as well. More bombs went off.

Suddenly, she heard steps approaching her position. The door opened slowly, and Slugger and Big Ben stepped inside. The giant was now in possession of the security manager's sawed-off shotgun, and he was still looking down. Slugger socked him in the chest. "Chin up!" he barked, and Ben slowly lifted his gaze.

"What are you doing?" shouted the emissary.

"Burning this place," answered the warlord calmly. She had no reply but shock and horror. "You and your kind should leave this world."

"But . . . we are helping."

"No . . . no, you're not."

"I . . . I helped you get your friend back!" The Vagantem was angry, and she stepped closer to them once she remembered she was protected in a suit of armor. A slim focus canon emerged from her chest and began to glow red, charging. It seemed her facial tentacles were controlling something below the visibility of the helmet.

The giant dropped the shotgun and swung his mace. The spike-less metal sphere rammed against the clear plastic of her helmet before her weapon was able to discharge. The plastic shattered and she wobbled to the ground. The alien technology sputtered, spitting sparks and beeping warning signals.

"Shhh," the warlord whispered as Ben slammed the mace down until death and destruction was ensured. The two then soaked the building in gasoline before exiting and tossing a match behind them. With the blood moon looming and the cherished screams of retribution ringing, Slugger found a porch across the street. He rushed to the steps and collapsed, trying to laugh off his nervous shakes. As he lay there calming himself down, he slipped into a memory dream as lucid as the present.

"Mom! I'm 'bout to head out. Where are you?" a young man ready for college called. He ran down the stairs, dragging a suitcase behind him. His mother met him by the door with a teary smile and a red nose.

"Do you have your toothbrush, phone charger, wallet, and computer?" she asked, sniffling.

The boy chuckled. "Yes, Mom," he said, annoyed yet warm.

"Do you have enough underwear and socks?"

"Yes, Mom," he said, this time more tenderly. She smiled, and more tears ran down her soft, rosy cheeks.

"I love you . . . I love you so, so much."

"I love you too, Mom."

She grabbed him by the face. "You . . . you are going to do so much for this world." They locked eyes until a series of mini-earthquakes roared and reality reemerged. Slugger looked out and saw a Vagantem warrior charging them, armor red as the moon.

"Come on!" he commanded as he dashed in the opposite direction. Big Ben stayed right behind him. Around the corner, one of his men waited in a stolen police cruiser. "Go!" he ordered as they jumped in. Despite the siren blaring, they couldn't steer out of the way of every citizen. Some were rammed aside, and a few were trampled, presumably killed. "Where's Pyro?"

"He said there should be more," answered the driver.

"More what?" asked the panting warlord.

"More fire."

During the commotion, they crashed into a telephone pole, but luckily for them, the front two airbags deployed, and Ben was all but indestructible, silent in the back. The smoke in the streets was now heavy and thick.

They exited the cruiser and continued their escape. A giant beaver the size of a pony bounded past them. Slugger watched it go and smiled. The smaller facilities had been unleashed. The plan was in motion, and they were headed to execute the next step.

As they moved, the attack continued all around them. Riots and looters—as predicted—soon filled the streets. The alien authorities began seizing the arsonists, terrorists, and trouble-makers along with innocent civilians caught in the crossfire.

Eventually, Slugger, Ben, and Kraven arrived at the Odyssey Sun Zoo and Aquarium; the last of the holding facilities. They hid behind a few bushes, protected by a knee-high gate. A few nervous guards had remained stationed there after others had fled. They shooed a tiger away with their gunfire. With the men was a Vagantem drone circling the air and shooting a spotlight about. "We'll go around. This way," said Slugger.

"Wait, Boss," mumbled Kraven. "The beasts will have to go through here. Better we make it clear."

Slugger nodded. "You got any suggestions?"

"Let's call up Java," Kraven mumbled.

The warlord pulled out a radio from a set taken from the farm. After tuning it, he spoke. "Java, it's Slugger . . . over."

After some cracks and pings, Java answered. "Hey Boss. The carnage is beautiful from up here."

"I bet it is. Can you see the Odyssey Sun Zoo and Aquarium? It's close to the center, but toward the northeastern side?"

"I'm looking . . . I'm looking. I don't think . . . wait! I see a zoo, but it looks like I only have a view of the back area. Are you inside?"

Slugger gritted his teeth. If he'd spent more time planning and studying this place, he could have set up Java in a more useful position. "No. We're at the entrance." Suddenly, the Vagantem drone stopped patrolling and aimed its spotlight beam in the direction of Slugger and his group. The warlord swallowed.

A shot sounded through the radio from Java's side, followed by a murderous chuckle. "I've taken down three of those floating robot orbs already." Slugger had no reply; he was still staring intently at the drone no more than fifty feet ahead of him. Ben and Kraven stared as well. Plasma pulses sounded through the static before cutting off. The warlord looked down at the radio, then back up at the drone, which was hovering its way over.

"Java?" There was no response.

"Humans! Step outside!" snapped the drone.

Before any of them could reply, Ben flung his mace through the brush. It cartwheeled in the air and whacked the drone. The drone dropped but ushered itself back into hovering mode before crashing. The spotlight now flickered, but a focus cannon emerged from its bottom, curving upward like a wasp's stinger. Multiple shots sprayed from multiple weapons. First, from Slugger's Berretta that he had so longed to use again, then Kraven's rifle, and lastly Ben's stolen shotgun. The drone plummeted, landing with a small explosion. The broken machine then bled blue flame.

"Let's go!" barked Slugger. His thoughts were heavy with loss already. No one had eyes like Java.

The group approached the front entrance of the zoo. It was short and wide, with a long gate that had bars shaped like the crowns of palm trees and grassland blades. A giraffe made of wire and twisted metal welcomed its arrivals from between two potted bushes. They could see no guards, assumed they must have left in the commotion, and continued on.

Then a voice boomed from the shadows, "Keep stepping closer if you wanna die tonight!"

The three intruders froze. Suddenly, a blistering explosion made them all tremble. It had come from inside the zoo. One guard revealed himself, only to run away frantically. The one who had spoken remained hidden somewhere in the shadows. "What do you want!" he demanded.

"I want many things, my friend. Tonight, I want fire and blood." Slugger's air was confident, despite his shaky hands and racing eyes. Fear pumped through his blood like a drug. "Save yourself, if you can." A second explosion popped off within the zoo, this time closer to the entrance. The guard bolted out into the street, drenched with desperation. Slugger chuckled. The three of them peered into the zoo through the gate but could not see through the smoke. Yowls and guttural roars chorused all around.

"Open it up," ordered the warlord.

Kraven, a burly man with a grizzly brown and grey beard and covered with muscle and grime, pulled out a pair of goggles and strapped them on. In the same bag he carried a portable welding torch wrapped around a small tank of gas. "Heh, I thought I'd be using this on that pipe bridge."

"You will," Slugger assured him. Ben and Slugger watched their surroundings as Kraven cut into the gate, burning a perfect entryway. Up ahead was the guard's box. Inside, they flipped a switch and the long entrance gate wheeled open along its tracks. Suddenly, a singed man with leathery skin and a slightly squinted eye panted up behind them.

"Where were you?" demanded Slugger.

Pyro laughed. "Fire . . . more fire." Slugger could not help but smirk.

"He came with the original group, right?" asked Kraven. The warlord nodded. "Then how is he more prepared than those of us who came after?"

Slugger shrugged. "Pyro's never without his satchel . . . his little devices."

Kraven looked over at the burnt man. His smile was mischievous, and snug in his arms was a pack that he cradled like a newborn.

"There's something you gotta see," said Pyro in a scratchy whisper.

They went deeper into the facility, passing splayed corpses

of both men and beasts. An elephant charged through smoke in the distance and fell down into the pit of another creature.

The aquarium was a long tunnel that snaked through several sections and ecosystem exhibits. The first few were cracked and drained, with rotting mulch and pools of still and muddy waters in the corners. The next few were full of dark, murky waters that teemed with death and decay. The last section was the only one still glowing with life. Fish and eels painted the liquid, shimmering bright colors off their scales. A hammerhead shark slowly swam right above them before jerking and shooting off in the opposite direction.

The anxious movement caught the men's attention, and they looked up. A dark shape swirled around, obscured by seaweed and air bubbles. The dark shape stopped above them while the four looked up in awe.

Claws gripped the glass. Only the tail swayed in the flow of the water. The men could now make out a pair of shoulders and a blunt, featureless face. Green eyes glared back at them, and a maw suddenly opened unnaturally wide. A large grey tongue emerged and flared out into a star-shaped sucker that blocked its face from view. The sucker began to try and rupture the glass. Slugger, Ben, Pyro, and Kraven quickly shoveled along, refusing to look up into the swimming horrors until they exited the tunnel.

Pyro led them to a section previously blocked by yellow tape; the yellow and black strips now either swayed in the dusty wind or lay defeated on the asphalt. A group of very large shipping containers sat beyond the perimeter of tape. The one in the center rattled, and a wet breath spewed through the bars at one end of the container. Whatever was inside was large and ferocious. The warlord looked at his welder and cranked his head toward the shipping container, signaling him to get to work.

Kraven stepped up reluctantly and began blasting the multiple padlocks and chains that locked the grated entrance. Suddenly, a terrible roar pummeled the man as spit and bloody dribble blasted his face. He jumped back and dropped his torch. After catching his breath, he grabbed his bolt cutters to finish the job. Once the gate was loose, Slugger and his men ran as far and as fast as they could into the night, giggling like spoiled children.

The shipping container was silent, and from inside, a monster nudged against the gate. It resisted slightly, but when the beast used all its weight with the second nudge, it flew open wildly, flinging bits of chain and lock all around. Out came a denizen of old Earth; a great behemoth of an ancient and primeval era. It had a slim, elongated snout ridged with sharp spears of teeth, eyes like a cat, and a great sail of a spine spotted with orange and purple. Three-pronged claws dangled from short arms. It stood on two powerful legs and was covered in a pale feathery fur.

The *Spinosaurus* sang a bloodcurdling cry to the moon before charging into the city's mayhem.

* * *

Ceteris was late. Although he had not known when exactly Slugger and his group would attack, he should have been ready. He had tried to visit the Huntress before the attack and was caught in the chaos.

He'd already recalled his wing; it had failed to find her, and he could not check on her now. He had a mission, and it was time sensitive.

When he finally reached the prison, he could see even from down the street that it had been shut down. The Vagantem quickened his pace, and as he neared, his interface chattered insistent warnings and highlighted a figure in his peripheral. The general turned to face it, proud and bold. The *Spinosaurus* shrieked its death call and dashed toward the alien, shaking the ground with each step.

Ceteris charged both his frontal focus cannon and his hulking shoulder turret. His suit began to sing, steam, and buzz, and then he discharged the weapons. The shoulder turret's double muzzle released two pulsating bolts of white-blue plasma that tore chunks out of the creature's sail. The frontal focus cannon zapped the dinosaur's chest with a continuous red laser, which seemed to have little effect. It staggered but soon corrected its course toward the alien.

Ceteris began to charge his weapons again, but the *Spinosaurus* had already reached him. The monster was easily twice his mech's size. It lunged and clamped its jaws down on Ceteris's arm as he raised it. Metal crunched between teeth and a blue liquid began to ooze from his suit. The *Spinosaurus* seemed repulsed by the battery fluid and let go immediately.

Ceteris's arm was now crushed and useless, but he managed to extend a dark silver blade from the wrist of his other arm. The creature spun and smacked him with its immense tail before he could do anything, throwing the warrior a good ten feet back. He clambered back up, weakened but determined. His shoulder cannon had been damaged in the tumble, and its aim was off; it fired into a burning building instead of at the dinosaur. Ceteris's focus cannon, however, fired and hit its target. The laser beam was able to pierce through the creature's skull, through its eye and into its brain. Smokey blood bubbled from the entrance wound. The dinosaur moaned before falling and shaking the earth for the last time.

Ceteris shuffled to the prison and slammed on the door. *"It is Ceteris! Let me in!"* After a few moments, the door was unlocked and lifted from the other side. Ceteris stormed in, wounded and half broken. Two Vagantem met him, while the sally port filled with guards.

"You leaving was poorly timed. Did you find what you set out for?" asked one of the Vagantem who squatted low beside a suited warrior. This unique Vagantem wore a dignified stardust coat along with a strange helmet-like cap that had many extensions and precise metal arms atop it. The twitching arms carried surgical tools, eyeglasses, and an assortment of other nameless instruments. His breathing apparatus did not hinder his speech.

"It does not matter. I apologize for taking up time and bringing you into this," Ceteris replied respectfully. The other Vagantem who had greeted Ceteris analyzed his damaged armor. Her coat, glimmering like the others, was large with many pockets. A pyramidal drone small enough to fit inside her pockets floated by her, tethered to her movements. *"Pax, Rada . . . come with me."*

"Do you not need to exit your armor?" she asked as Ceteris's suit began to sputter.

"Come." Ceteris ignored her. As he approached the lead guard, he waited for him to bow low, but he didn't. *"Who am I to you? Was I not once a general, deserving of respect?"*

"Once, perhaps." The guards were suited in the more recent bloodsilver mechs, which outperformed Ceteris's sunmetal tech even at full functionality. The guard leader's eyes were

angry and flecked with stars and sparks. *"This is all because of you, and him. The ship too, wasn't it? You have no regard for the innocents caught between. You and that prisoner will commit far worse atrocities in the name of what? Revenge? Spite? You call him pool swimmer and traitor. You are worse . . . in every way."* Ceteris remained silent, staring back with white-pricked eyes. *"Rada, Pax . . . you have not yet committed treason. Be mindful of your families, and your lives."*

"What families? Do you know what goes on up there . . . guard?" hissed the female Vagantem. *"Death crawls all about the hulls. Disease, depression, boiling resentment. What do you know of how families hold on up there? Everyone is scattered, waiting for death under him. Auroron is nothing but a failure who equates the Critori, and even these humans, with us."*

"Are they really any worse than us?" asked the guard.

"That matters little. What matters is what priorities our leader should have. Us. The Vagantem. We could have been far from here, discovering countless worlds and stars. Or we could have created an actual home for us here. Instead we float above a hellish abyss, in limbo, and squander every sinew of potential we ever muster. Our people are in decay. Our society and culture is now all but dead. Art and recreation have become distant dreams. Families are diminished, many turning back to the old gods of Vaga. Some Vagantem are even turning to the Critori Lunar Brotherhood and their dark, primitive ways. No one agrees on what to do; no one is civil or caring anymore. We need direction and true leadership, a goal, a vision, a united front. I followed Auroron, same as you. I believed in him, I trusted him . . . I helped vote him in. That Vagan is not just corrupt—he is delusional and shortsighted. He is not fit to lead," said Rada, the female Vagantem accompanied by her small floating drone.

"And that prisoner will bring us a better future?" the guard scoffed and his tentacles flicked upward inside his helmet. *"You are the ones who are delusional. How many more will die? Do you tell yourselves every day that you are heroes and patriots?"* The lead guard stepped up, threateningly. *"I do not agree with everything he does, but Auroron is a good Vagan. Not a cruel murderous blackheart like that thing down in the cell. I've let you visit here because I actually pitied you. Wearing that obsolete golden mech, even as it fails you now, even when you lost the title of general. You're pathetic, and you will never see the top of my head!"*

"Where is the warden?" asked Ceteris, solemn.

"In hiding, like a coward," barked the guard.

"I see. End him," ordered Ceteris. Suddenly, two guards grabbed their captain, ripped his shoulder turret off, and forced him to his knees. There was only one in the group of guards besides the captain who resisted, and he began a heavy and metallic wrestle with another. *"This way,"* Ceteris muttered to Pax and Rada, paying no heed to the tussle of armored hulks in the sally port.

Ceteris struggled as they darted down the dark hallways, and Rada watched him in concern. A plasma blast echoed from behind and Pax turned in dismay. All he could see was dim black. The trio hurried until they reached the final cell. A silent guard stood before the gate, lowering his head and waiting for Ceteris to release him. The ex-general placed his right hand atop the guard's helmet and allowed him to rise. *"Saj Geevorensy."* Ceteris was stern. The guard's eyes widened upon hearing his name.

"Yes, Prime General?"

"Come." The guard followed. He opened the cell once they reached it, and chains rolled on the ground. Then came

gargling and spitting. *"Nes!"* Ceteris shouted as he charged into the shadowed cage to find his brother.

"General . . . never worry for me," slithered Nes. *"Pax, Rada . . . Saj. Thank you for being here."*

"You will still need to recover in a lab after this. Have you been breathing this air?" asked Pax Leosine.

"Sometimes. They left a stationary breather with me." Nes motioned with his shriveled and exposed arm toward a metal instrument sticking out of the ground with tanks of gas ringed around it. Vagantem symbols and images were printed onto the glass vials bundled atop the tanks. The breathing tube was short. Ceteris's mech gave off a glow, dimmer than the guard's, allowing the unarmored to see just enough.

Rada Phasm stepped up without a word. Her drone spat light and revealed Nes Bossvan. His skin was patched with black and silver flesh, and his eyes were black with dying stars in the corners of his irises. Thick metal rings covered the tentacles around his mouth. They seemed tight, while the flesh in between throbbed above the metal. Chains wrapped the creature and weighed down every movement. *". . . He kept you in here? Like this?"* she said in shock. Nes only looked back. There was a pride inside him still; pride that refused defeat.

"Pax, Rada, please . . . get these off of him," pleaded Ceteris. Rada was ready and inched closer immediately, examining Nes's facial tendrils. Pax, however, remained. Ceteris and the guard turned to face him, not in intimidation, but in confusion.

"I'm afraid I must ask something. As well as demand," Pax Leosine said, his voice harsh as he squared his shoulders.

"Demand?" Ceteris seethed.

"What is this question? And then we can talk about this demand," said Nes.

"They are tied. My demand is that you answer the question truthfully," said Pax. Silence answered and Pax asked his question. *"Was it your plot to destroy the capital ship?"*

"No . . . we believe the Lunar Brotherhood is attempting to frame us," Nes said swiftly. Pax's tentacles curled up, and then slowly unraveled.

"I'm sure it would please you to know that many believe this . . . or, the other misguided notion that it is a plot by the Cri-Shaw Tori and Auroron himself to tighten their control. Have you yourself sewn dissent . . . or was it just the administration's failings? No . . . it was neither." Pax strolled by Ceteris and the guard until he met Nes face-to-face. *"It has been so long . . . the reason you are here, I think, is a farse. Seeing you in here, like this, further sours my feelings toward the star teller. I never liked him. I thought he was eccentric and blind, and—as Rada says—shortsighted. My family looked fondly upon your reign. Still . . . one hundred seventy-one thousand and forty-four. That is how many Vagan died on that ship. Innocent lives caught in a conflict they did not want any part of. My cousins were among them. The Lunar Brotherhood lost many in that ship as well. No big names for your spies to tell you, but enough to make an impact. Tell me . . . truthfully . . . how do you expect me to follow a liar?"*

The other Vagantem all swayed their eyes back to Nes, awaiting his answer. *"Pax. You are just like your father. And your mother. You've taught me a valuable lesson; one as leader I shall never forget. I will never take your loyalty for granted again."*

"Was it you?" Pax asked again.

"Yes," answered Nes.

"How? Why?"

"He was supposed to be on that ship."

"But he wasn't."

"Did you get a glimpse of the city? Before this attack, of course," asked Nes, but none answered. *"A true monument to his work. No real progress being made. Fathomless resources squandered on these pitiful people. And for what? So he could marvel at them like the creatures he breeds in labs? So he could tend to his curiosity instead of his people's hopes?"*

"He does not kill his own," Pax pointed out.

"Are you sure? If he is not out of office soon, our people will be lost forever. Our journey will end. I will live with what I've done until the Sun Mother casts me out into oblivion, but the Vagan race will soar and live with the stars."

"Do you sleep?" asked a now pitiful Pax.

"I will never sleep again," answered Nes grimly.

"You must make it right. Lead our people. Be honest with them. We will find glory again."

"They cannot know," said Ceteris.

"Not yet," agreed Pax.

"You made your decision the moment you decided to come down here with me. We must get to it, now!" barked Rada.

The multi-tooled cap upon Pax's head began to twitch and shift, switching through items like a band of swiss army knives. He examined the skin and flesh while Rada studied the rings. *"These are dead stars. They would have disintegrated you if you had left this cage,"* said Rada. Her drone flew circles around the patient, scanning the devices attached to him.

"Yes, I've heard of these. The guards made sure I knew not to try," said Nes as his vision angled upward. An intricate surgery was then performed, with both medical and technical expertise, as the city burned outside.

Chapter XIII – Homeward Bound

The morning was pink and late. Smoke gathered in the sky, though the fires were all but out. A Vagantem ship hovered over the skyscrapers, releasing an army of smaller ships and drones that flew down upon the wreckage. The ship resembled a black crossbow bolt with long quills running down its spine. Wails and moans of monsters below were scarce but still present. Most of the creatures had been recaptured, maimed, or put down; others had escaped. The cries of the injured had persisted through the night and still pierced the air.

In the distance, the Huntress limped away from the city. She turned one last time to look at New Blake-Shire, now no more. She had new scars, and black dirt and smut framed her face. She had nothing with her but her spear; she had not been ready and left in a hurry. Away she went, headed for a friend's.

She approached the farm, and while she had no radio to warn the snipers, she still expected a warm welcome. However, before she arrived at the orchard, she noticed that the farm was deathly quiet. The atmosphere was aloof. Something was not right, and she couldn't bear it. She paused before going any further, but it was too late. From afar, she made out men, and then more, and soon realized she was surrounded by encroaching hostiles. One shape stuck out in particular, the largest shape among them: Ben.

"Where's your cat?" The Huntress watched Slugger emerge from behind the giant as he asked. His smile was dirty and stained and smug. The wild in his eyes flickered, and she no longer liked it as she did before. She gave no answer. "Aww . . . what's wrong?" the warlord taunted.

"Shut up, you fuckin' worm!" She ground her teeth and her blood roared in her ears.

The surrounding marauders laughed as they approached. "Oooh, this one's mine." One blurted out as he reached out to grab her by the butt. She twisted immediately, swinging an elbow and breaking the man's front teeth. He fell back and the laughter grew.

"Don't touch me. I am no one's!"

The warlord stepped up, putting aside his evil smirk for a moment. "First of all, I would never disrespect you like that. Second . . . you are mine . . . because everything in this fucking world . . . is mine. Now, you better come to terms with that, and you better do it fast." Their eyes locked and dueled, then hers quelled. Her eyes glazed as Slugger moved the group along.

A fire pit blazed, and the men sat around it. The Huntress was tied up, but left alone. They were deep in the green jungle, just before the rocky plateau that led back to his wasteland and canyon. Some of the men were proud and rambunctious, singing tales of victory and glory. Others were quiet and sad, fevered with loss. Slugger stood up to speak aloud. His aura was cold.

"Java had the greatest eyes of any rifleman. He was a master, and an artist. Noodle always made me laugh. He was the king of chefs, and I promised him an upgraded kitchen, but never got to it. Cass was loyal and smart, never questioning, always going the extra mile. Bones too. I remember Bones saved my life once, from some sniveling pussy who tried to stab me in the back. Duke and Stew were best friends, ever since they were kids. I don't know if any of you knew this, but they were. Their friendship was one of the strongest bonds I'd ever seen. These men are irreplaceable. Their legacy is left with us, and we will honor them." The warlord began to think of Willie, but could not bring himself to say anything. He dug into his pocket to make sure the wooden carving Willie had left behind was still there.

The night rolled on and morning hit them like a dreadful hangover. On the move again, they trudged. They climbed, slow and careful, tying themselves to jagged rocks and grabs. The cliff had treacherously steep areas, but also natural steps and layered ledges that made half the climb easier. The Huntress was strapped tightly to Ben's back, her feet dangling like a child's. The cast on one foot was dirty and battered and had begun to unravel. Slugger smiled at that, thinking back to when he was in a similar position. The moment was short-lived, and he grew bored of waiting for her to catch his smile.

Once they reached the top, the men took in the scenery. The sky was a clear blue with a white sun and specks of clouds here and there. The empty wasteland seemed to stretch out forever. The ground was broken and parched, and very few weeds shifted with the wind where they stuck out of cracks and holes in the dry, hardpacked earth. It was welcoming to the men, but menacing and hopeless to the Huntress.

The group was as thirsty as the ground, and even hungrier. They had depleted all their supplies, and had not stopped to hunt or gather. Slugger had spotted a dying creek in the jungle, and they were able to take some water, but that was soon depleted as well. When they reached the cavernous split of the crack, they looked all about for the bridge and their vehicles and argued for an hour on whether to go left or right. They chose left, and luckily were right.

The bridge remained, and more vehicles were now there than when Slugger and the initial group had departed on foot. Looking at his truck, the warlord thought of the cage he'd had Ben knock down into the crack. He wished he'd kept it now. The Huntress was put in the truck while Canada accompanied her, holding a barrel to her head. The convoy revved and gusted a sandy wind behind it. Home was but a charge away.

They continued riding in the night, stampeding through the cold open wastes. Their headlights lifted the near darkness and glared like owl eyes. As dawn emerged, so did the canyon, in all its glory. Men were already working high on the upper levels while others scurried about down below, ready to start the day.

"Canada, Pyro, Moose . . ." Slugger turned to these three. "Please, I need you for one more thing." They all nodded. These men, he knew, were unlike most; his shadow knights, he sometimes called them, along with Jim, Willie, and very few others. The existence of this group and its purpose were a secret. Those who belonged to it had proven themselves the most loyal time and time again. He could entrust his life to them, and he would allow them to challenge and sway him. He loved them, and they loved him. "And Brody. You too."

"Yes, sir."

Brody was not yet a member. None of those outside the shadow knights knew of the group and therefore did not know how to join. Brody had been close to becoming a part of this secret operation for some time, but after this, Slugger would make sure to cement his position in the group. He would not say anything now, though. Not all the shadow knights knew the full extent of the group and how many were involved. It was more of a tally locked inside the warlord's head.

"The rest of you. Go home. Get some rest. Everyone will hear of what you've done, and you will be rewarded. Thank you." Ben was the only one who remained aside from the others Slugger had asked to stay. "You should rest, big guy," he said to the giant. Ben remained silent and still. Slugger cracked a smirk. "Alright, alright. Come on," he said after roughly patting him on the back.

Slugger and Ben took the truck, while Canada kept watch over the Huntress in the back. The others were close behind in a beaten-up minivan with off-road tires. They headed south, toward the forest, the Huntress bleakly quiet since her capture.

The day ended just as they reached the border. The trees and plants were naked and sparse, but soon turned vibrantly colorful with the coming of night. They set up a fire and loosened the Huntress's rope restraints, allowing her to sit on a log and take in some warmth. Slugger scooted closer. She remained sightless and uncaring.

"We visited your place during the commotion, but no one was home. What happened to your cat?" he asked.

She looked at him scornfully. "Jumped out of my arms and I lost her as we tried to run."

Slugger nodded sadly. "I know what that feels like." She only looked at him confused, irritated almost. "That is the reason I came down to that farm in the first place."

". . . Why?"

"Because of this . . ." She had almost forgotten about it:

the decorated rifle, and now the dreadful sense that she was somehow responsible for what had occurred in New Blake-Shire and the farm sat on her shoulders, stomping out the bitter denial. Slugger ran his finger along the set of teeth situated on the gun, before petting the bony snout. ". . . this is Homer." The Huntress could then guess what had happened.

"The poachers?" she presumed. Slugger bit his lip, and for some reason, that was an answer she understood. She wondered what part Ceteris had played in all of this, suddenly reminded of his vague request. "Where are you taking me?"

Slugger didn't answer until she repeated herself.

"To meet someone."

* * *

A strange tree stood out, as if it didn't belong. The bark was a silver-blue, covered in holes, and cracked with lines splintering at the edges. The leafless branches curved and noodled amongst themselves. Slouching at its base was a cabin with missing planks. It was old but strong; lost and forgotten, but ever resistant. Slugger and Ben approached with their captive. The Huntress was mostly free aside from her wrists being roped together. The giant carried both his mace and her spear. The rest of the small group remained back to watch the vehicles by a creek that allowed them to recuperate.

So, it was just the three of them until they were suddenly met by another group of three. The warlord grinned so wide his face started to warm and ache.

"Slugger!"

"Boss!"

"Slug!"

Three young boys ran up to the warlord as if they were seeing their hero for the first time, giddy and unable to quell their excitement. Billy, the blonde with his backward cap. Rudy, the redhead with freckles and a shirt too small for his gut. And Louis, peering through foggy glasses and greasy black hair. The kids were survivors, each holding tools of violence. Billy with his pickaxe, Rudy with his machete, and Louis with his AK-47. "The mighty Lost Boys, in the flesh." He welcomed them with respect.

"What are you doing here?" Rudy asked in a manner that seemed to suggest this place was not good enough for the warlord.

"To see you. Where's Talia?"

Talia exited the cabin, and it was clear she had been listening in. She did not seem as happy as the others to see their leader, and her brown piercing eyes were glued to the Huntress. She removed her woolen beanie and pulled down the black bandana that covered her face, revealing her olive skin and letting her space-black hair flow down fluidly.

"Who is she?" Her words bubbled with rage. The boys grew nervous as one leader challenged another.

Slugger scoffed. He strolled up to meet Talia, his protege. As he looked down at her with a crazed look, Talia did not falter, instead lifting her chin to meet his gaze. Before he said anything, Slugger suddenly wrapped his arms around her, then squeezed and lifted her up. He spun her around and the other boys laughed. This took the Huntress by surprise. "I missed you, you fuckin' brat."

"Put me down!"

"Not 'til you hug me back." For a split second, the Huntress caught a repressed smile, and the shimmering of a tear being built up in the young girl's ducts. Talia then squeezed him back. "Alright, alright! Enough," said the warlord as he dropped her roughly, though the girl was able to plant her feet and catch herself. She wiped her tears and cleared her throat, resuming the angry tone.

"Who is she?" Talia persisted.

"Where are the twins?" the warlord asked.

"Out," she spat and resumed waiting for the answer to her previous question.

"Call her Huntress," answered Slugger as he prompted the woman to walk up. The Huntress stared down at the girl in wonder.

"Why is she here . . . and why is she fucking looking at me like that?"

"Calm down, Talia. I need you to show her around the forest . . . teach her the laws of my land; the land that will one day be yours." He gave her a wink, then looked over to the confused woman. "You are a free citizen now," he said with a quick laugh. "You *were* dead in my mind already . . . I was gonna flay you, keep you alive for a screaming bit. And I'm not exactly sure what happened. These kids would know; I got a fucking weak spot, I'm a goddamn pushover . . . am I right?"

"Ehh, sometimes," answered Billy.

The warlord's face then went emotionally barren, and he grew deadly serious. "You know where I am. The canyon. You can be a part of it too, but I'm not gonna force you there. Take your time. Taste this part of the world, and maybe we'll see each other again." Big Ben tossed her spear into the dirt for her to recover. "Lastly, Talia is in charge. You give any of my Lost Boys the slightest bit of trouble, and the hunt is on for you; the last hunt. I will make you eat your own skin." Then he looked back at the group of young ones with a twinkle. "Though . . . they don't really need my protection or my threats anymore."

* * *

For many months, Slugger's canyon fortress enjoyed relative peace. They conducted a ceremony for the slain, their fallen brethren. Trade, infrastructure, expansion, and morale was on the rise.

The warlord rubbed his erect phallus as he looked out from his dark, crooked tower onto everything he had built and defended. Jim approached from behind, his vest and shirt rising above his tattooed belly. "Haven't heard any cries or tail smacks in a while," he said with satisfaction.

"She's gettin' better. I might now have some competition for her love though," said the warlord suggestively. Jim smirked, embarrassed.

"Yeah, we're friends now. I fell asleep with her in her cage the first week you were gone, but she missed you. Don't be jealous," Jim joked.

Slugger scoffed, warmheartedly. "Fuck off already." Jim chuckled, then left after a friendly grip on his leader's shoulder.

The warlord wallowed in his self-reflection, thinking of all the events that had recently transpired. He was at peace but on edge at the same time, and it was inexplicable.

Suddenly, peace was lost, the sense of calming days dissipated, and the cries for war rang out from below. Above, many black shapes were clustering in the sky, casting shadows down upon the sunny wastes. Ships, alien ships, were all about. The warlord crunched his teeth, nipping off a small piece of lip without notice. He started to shake the rails he was holding on to.

Men from the upper levels shot futilely toward the invading Vagantem, but the ships were too strong. A rocket launcher was fired, and Slugger followed the trail of smoke back to the entrance gate and found Moose commanding his team. The missile hit the biggest ship and splattered flame about its face. The ship wiggled in the air and small cracks appeared, though it managed to stabilize.

Suddenly, a booming command blared from the fleet's speakers. "Humans . . . hold your fire." It was English, but the words did not come from a human.

"Stop!" ordered Slugger, and those that heard him pointed upward at him, and soon the swaths of people in the canyon obeyed his command. Drones spilling out of other ships surrounded the hit ship, spraying white foam on the fire and administering in-flight repairs. Once the damaged ship was taken care of, the fleet began its descent. What surprised Slugger the most was how the ships all crowded up outside his front gate, almost respectfully, not daring to land inside his borders. They now waited for him, the man in charge.

The drawbridge gate rolled open and slammed the earth. Hollow skulls on the railheads looked down at their visitors. Slugger emerged, with Big Ben, Jim, Moose, Pyro, Canada, Brody, and many, many others behind him. More were stationed on the upper levels.

The main ship was long and bullet-shaped, with two sets of tripod legs, one in the front and another in the back. It was smooth with little detail on the outside plating. A door slid open and leaked white light, even brighter than the blistering sun above. Slugger was seething and blood trickled down his lip where he'd bitten the small chunk off.

A long ramp glissaded out before the tip of the tongue dug into the hard, dry earth. Stairs then raised from the ramp. Various Vagantem sentries and officials emerged at the top of the ramp. They grouped in formation, lining up in rows as they waited for another to exit.

When he finally did, all fell silent. A strange Vagantem, tall and slender as a man with a straightened spine, walked down gracefully. His arms were crossed behind his back. The alien was dressed in a black suit with an ocean-green tie. He stopped at the end of the ramp, as if he as well was waiting for another.

Slugger's eyes swelled in disgust at this alien figure, but something else quickly made him forget. The warlord's jaw dropped and he froze in utter shock; he couldn't move or even hear anything. The next figure to exit the ship and walk slowly down the ramp was a man; a familiar man. An ebony man with eyes that bore through Slugger. He too was clean and wearing a suit. Yet, the man had two arms—as did most men—but . . . was he supposed to?

Everything came back to him once he found the name in his memory. "Shane."

Shane looked over at the tall Vagantem and nodded before approaching Slugger alone. Slugger stopped any who tried to follow him as he moved toward Shane, and the two met, face-to-face, with their respective factions behind them.

"You found a ladder. How does it feel to betray your own race? Better yet . . . what the fuck is that thing doing in people clothes?" the warlord asked, but Shane did not answer. "Finally come to kill me then?"

Shane's eyes were cool, but Slugger caught a slight anxious twitch in them. "We're not here for that." The man's words were careful and clear of any passion.

Slugger smirked. "Oh no? Then what are you here for?" he taunted.

Shane's sight lost its grip and seemed aimless. He was obviously in deep thought, and he looked like Atlas with the weight of the world on his shoulders. "We need your help." And there it was, rage submerged, exposed through his words like a ruptured pipe, or leak of lava. Slugger smiled again, the thin bloody trail still running down his chin.

". . . Seriously?"

Made in the USA
Monee, IL
29 October 2020

46358521R00095